ACCIDENTAL LOVE

LK

Contents

1
THE ACCIDENT

Raj, a man with a six-foot figure, wearing expensive clothes and his face expressionless, was standing outside a mansion, waiting impatiently for his driver. After about 5 minutes a car arrived, and he sat inside.

"Uncle, you are late again. If you continue to be late every day, then I am sorry, but I will have to find a new driver.", said Raj.

"I am really sorry Mr. Raj. I promise it won't happen again." The driver replied.

"Hmmm. Now take me to the factory."

"Yes sir." After a boring drive that lasted thirty minutes, they reached the factory. Raj got out of the car and went inside the building. He saw the laborers working diligently, and after seeing all the processes being carried out smoothly, he went to the supervisor's cabin and found him sleeping.

" Mr. Sham, Mr. Sham wake up."

Mr. Sham woke up after hearing his name called out repeatedly and loudly. He saw his boss and stood up straight.

"G..g..good...good morning sir."

" Mr. Sham, I have had complaints against you accusing you of being careless and irresponsible. I didn't want to jump to conclusions without proof. So, I decided to check if the accusations were accurate, and it looks like they were. You are fired. I'd suggest you find a job that allows you to fulfill your requirement of rest. Now you may leave." Raj said in a finalizing tone. Mr. Sham knew better than to argue with his head. He tried to convince Raj by pleading to him and apologizing for sleeping when he should have been working. However, it all went in vain. And Mr. Sham was escorted out by the security guards. Raj called his father,

"Dad, I have fired Mr. Sham from our local factory. He was slacking in his work, and you know how much I hate that. Just appoint someone else and till the time you do so, send Rohit here, please. He can take charge."

" Okay Raj, as you say. I will do it. You should leave for your meeting now or else you will be late."

"Hmm. I will. Bye"

"Bye" Raj cut the call and left the factory. As soon as he sat in the car, he told his driver, "Uncle, please take me to the office now." The driver simply nodded and drove off. When he reached his office, he asked his driver to go back home and left for his cabin to collect some files. Once he was done, he went to the conference room. When he entered, he saw his client already present. He sat down. "Good afternoon, Mr. Sharma. How are you? I am sorry if you had to wait long. I was busy with some company matters." Raj greeted the man sitting in front of him.

" I am fine. How are you? And no need to apologize, we just got here so we didn't wait much."

" I am also fine. Thank you. Shall we start the meeting?"

"Yes please" Raj nodded and switched on the projector. He had prepared a presentation, with which he managed to impress his clients. Once he was finished, he received a huge round of applause.

" Thank you, thank you very much. So, what do you think of our company and our policies?"

"We are quite impressed, but we would need to discuss it before we tell you our final decision. As you are aware, this is a huge order as we need the uniforms for all of our staff as well as to give to charity. Therefore, it is not an easy decision to make."

"Sure sir, I understand. I will step out of the room."

After Raj was gone, Mr. Sharma and his partners talked for a few minutes and then invited Raj back in. Once he entered, Mr. Sharma said, " We think that this company has great potential and that if anyone should get our contract then it's you."

" Thank you for giving us the honor. We won't let you down." Raj thanked his clients profusely. They nodded and signed the contract. Everyone shook hands and left. Raj went to his cabin and called his parents to share the good news. " Mom, dad we did it. We just got the biggest contract yet of our lives."

"Congratulations Raj. We knew you could do it. Love you. Now quickly come home, I will make your favorite sweet dish." said his mother.

" Yes, congrats my boy. Now finish your work at the office and come home as soon as possible."

"Yes mom, yes dad. I will come after giving the instructions to the factory. Rohit is there, right?

" Yes." his dad answered.

" Okay. I will call him. Bye, love you both." He cut the call. He then dialed Rohit's number.

"Hey, bro. Guess what? I got the contract."

" Congrats bro. You better give me a party for it. Also send me the details and I will get the work started." "Cool. I will send you the contract right away but just so you know we have two months to complete this order. So, work on it accordingly. By the way, mom has made Halwa at home, so come fast."

"Okay, once I finish my work here, I will leave."

They talked some more and then ended the call. Raj sent the details of the order to his brother and then after informing the receptionist, he left for his home. He was going on his bike, since he had sent the driver back. He loved to ride during the evening, enjoying the open sky, feeling the cool wind on the skin of his forearms. Soon he reached home. He saw his parents waiting for him. He touched their feet, took their blessings and hugged them. They congratulated him on his achievement. After chatting for a few more minutes, he left for his room to change his clothes. When he came back, he saw that Rohit had still not come. He was surprised as the factory wasn't so far that it would take his brother so long to come home. With the thought that Rohit must be on his way, he ignored the feeling of worry and focused on enjoying the evening. He sat with his parents and waited for Rohit, but even after an hour there was no sign of his younger brother. He called Rohit again and again but each time the call went unanswered. The anxiety and the dreadful feeling of worry returned unavoidable this time. After about 10 minutes Raj's phone rang. The caller ID said it was Rohit. Raj immediately answered the call. "Hello. Rohit? Where are you? We are waiting since so long. What happened, why haven't you reached yet?"

"Hello?", an unfamiliar voice came from the phone. "Hello, actually there was an accident in which the owner of this phone was injured. He had probably been riding a bike and I don't know what exactly happened, but I found him unconscious and bleeding, so I brought him to the 'Safe n Care hospital'. I saw his phone and wanted to call his family to inform them about the accident. I saw many missed calls from this number and so I called back. Are you perhaps related to him?" Raj was shaken. He couldn't believe that his brother had been in an accident. He didn't want to believe. He decided to confirm that it was his brother only.

" Did you check the license number on the bike?"

" No, but I did notice the bike's design. It was red with streaks of white. And there was Ro written on one of the handlebars. Could you please tell me if you are a relative of the man?"

Raj was on the verge of crying. That was his brother's bike. They both had one, his was blue and was customized to have Ra written on the handlebar, while Rohit's was red and had Ro written instead. It was their birthday gift from their parents. What was supposed to be such a big day for him, and his family, had turned out to be one of the worst days of their lives. His brother had had an accident and was in the hospital, unconscious. He somehow controlled his emotions and said, "Yes, I am his brother. I will be reaching in 10 minutes. Please wait for me."

"Okay."

2
ATTEMPT TO MURDER

He cut the call and broke down. Seeing him cry his parents were confused. Nevertheless, they tried to comfort him, but he continued sobbing. He was the type of person who could stay calm in the toughest situations. He almost never cried so seeing him looking so devastated and unable to stop his tears, made them worried. They tried to ask him about the phone call, but he wasn't in a state to answer them. All of a sudden, he wiped away his tears, got up, took his car keys and left. Feeling perplexed, anxious and worried sick about their sons, his parents followed him. After a short drive, they found themselves in front of the hospital. Their anguish now increased, they went inside and saw Raj talking to a man.

"Excuse me, are you the one who called me? And informed me about my brother's accident?", Raj asked.

"Yes, I was the one who called you."

" Where is he? How is he? How did this happen? Could you please tell me?"

"He is in the ICU. I am not sure about his condition as the doctors haven't told me anything yet. I am not entirely sure how this happened, but I have called the police just in case. They must be on their way."

"Okay, thank you so much. I really can't express how thankful I am. If you ever need anything, anything just give me a call. Here is my card"

"It was my duty for the sake of humanity. If I ever need any help from you, I will be sure to ask. Thank you, but I should leave now. My wife must be waiting for me at home."

"Sure and thank you once again for all your help " The man smiled and nodded before leaving. Raj sighed and looked around. He saw his parents who were looking back at him. He got nervous. He didn't know how to break the news to them. How was he supposed to tell them that their son had been in an accident and was currently unconscious. Before he could even begin to explain the situation to them, two police officers came to him.

"Excuse me, do you know anyone by the name of Raj?", one of them asked. "

I am Raj. Are you the officers investigating Rohit's accident?"

"Actually, it wasn't an accident. Hello, I am Lieutenant Param and he is my partner Inspector Kehan."

They shook hands. Param continued speaking, " We don't think that it was an accident. It was a planned attempt to murder. There were cameras around the area where the incident occurred. We saw the footage. Mr. Rohit was stuck in traffic. He was in front of a jeep. When the traffic began to clear, the jeep that was behind him tried to move ahead. Your brother noticed and moved aside. The jeep should have had enough space to move without even touching the bike. However, as he started to go forward, the jeep shifted slightly, slamming against his bike, causing him to lose control and collide with the car in front of him. Toppling over the bike with him underneath. Had it not been for the gentleman who called us, your brother may as well have been there only, probably dead by now."

Raj was listening very carefully, but when the lieutenant said the last sentence, he looked up in shock. "Why would anyone want to kill him? What has he ever done?"

"Oh, he didn't need to do anything. If I am not wrong, you are the CEO of Malhotra Industries, right?" After Raj confirmed that he was indeed the CEO, Param continued, "Yes, and also you just got a very big order for your company just a few hours ago, am I right?"

Raj was astonished, " Yes, you are absolutely correct but how did you know?"

"How did we know? Sir, the whole world knows about it. Somehow, the media managed to get hold of this news and its spreading like wildfire." Kehan exclaimed.

Raj was taken aback. He looked at the senior officer to confirm. The office nodded his head in yes, confirming what Kehan had just said. Raj took a few deep breaths to calm himself down and asked the officers to continue.

"Well, seeing your success, anyone could get jealous and do something like this." Param explained.

"Jealous? If it was jealousy, then I should have been the victim not my brother. Do you even know what you are saying?" Raj busted upon the Lieutenant. After a minute of silence, he apologized,

"I am sorry, it's just that I have been on edge since I got the news of my brother.". "It's ok Mr. Malhotra. we understand. And as for why Mr. Rohit was the victim instead of you, unfortunately right now, I do not have an answer. However, we are investigating the matter as top priority. We are currently looking for the driver of the jeep but it's taking some time because the license plate of the jeep was not that clear in the recordings. I am really sorry about your brother, but we must leave now. Please call us when he wakes up. We will have to question him. As soon as we find anything we will inform you."

Raj just nodded, too confused and emotional to speak. The officers left. Raj looked at his parents. They were coming to talk to him when the officers arrived, and they had heard everything. There were tears in their eyes. They looked back at Raj and beckoned him. Raj quickly went and hugged his mother and started crying badly.

"Mom, why him? Why? It should have been me instead. Not him" His mother tried to console him while crying uncontrollably herself. His father saw that and comforted his wife. Soon a doctor came out of the ICU. Raj saw this and got up. He removed the tears from his cheek and went up to the doctor.

"Doctor, how is my brother? Is he awake? He will be okay, right?"

"See, I will be honest with you. His condition is not that good. The bike fell on his chest, breaking a few bones. And there was a lot of blood loss too. We are trying our best, but he needs to be operated upon immediately. Sorry, we cannot share any more details as of yet. We have called our chief surgeon; you can talk to her once she is here. Only she can save him now."

3

DR. SEENA

"Then where is she? She is a doctor, right? Shouldn't she be here saving lives. What do you mean by you have called her? What if it's too late by the time she reaches? Who will be responsible? You?" Raj shouted. The doctor took a deep breath, glared at the people who had stopped to see the drama and calmly said,

"Mr. Raj, I understand your frustration, but please calm down. I assure you that Dr. Seena is on her way, and she is more than capable. She will do anything to save your brother. Please cooperate."

"Raj, calm down son. Nothing will happen to Rohit. Come here." Raj's father called out. Raj nodded and went to his parents. Five minutes later, a young, tall woman, wearing jeans and t-shirt, her hair tied in a high ponytail came there. She stopped at the reception and when the receptionist said something, she nodded looking at Raj and his family and then went towards them.

"Hi, I am Doctor Seena. You don't need to worry about anything. Rohit will be absolutely fine. I promise.", she assured them. Before anyone could say anything, the doctor who had called Seena came there,

" Doctor, the patient is critical. We have shifted him to the operating theatre. Please come fast." They left.

"What kind of a doctor is she? She came so late that my brother became critical. Her duty is to save lives, not put anyone's life in danger. If anything happens to him, I will not leave her."

Raj was very angry. After a pause, he said," Mom, he will be fine, right?"

"He will. He has to be." His mother tried to show the confidence which she herself was lacking. Nobody said anything anymore. All of them were tensed and were praying to God for Rohit's health. After about an hour, Seena came out of the operating theatre. Raj's dad saw her and immediately went to her.

" Doctor, how is my son? Is he fine?" Seena looked at him and smiled.

"He is absolutely fine."

Hearing this, Raj looked up. The whole family was relieved. Suddenly, Raj noticed a look of slight nervousness come on Seena's face.

"Is there anything wrong Dr. Seena?" Seena looked at him, closed her eyes and sighed. She looked at Raj's parents and said,

"There is one thing. Your son is out of danger. He will have to stay here for some time, in order to recover completely. The fractures in his chest should heal soon. Unfortunately, there is little chance that his legs will ever heal." The three of them were shook. "

So, you are saying that Rohit may never be able to walk again." Raj confirmed hoping the answer was no.

Seena looked him straight in the eye and simply shook her head in yes. Raj closed his eyes in an effort to stop the overflow of emotions inside him. " See, I know it must be hard for you all, but trust me I did my best. And honestly, it does not have to be that serious. I have seen innumerable cases like this. People, even though physically disabled, have achieved and fulfilled their dreams and they are living an almost completely normal life. Sure, it will take some time to adjust, but sooner or later, everything will be fine. Also, there is still a chance that he may be able to walk but that won't be at least for the next few years. So, you should not lose hope completely but at the same time it would be better for you to not have any high expectations. " Seena tried to comfort the family. Now Raj couldn't tolerate it anymore. The mere thought of the possibility of his brother never being able to walk again terrified him. He complained,

" You are a doctor. You are supposed to help him, and here you are telling us that it's not a big deal. He may never be able to walk again. Sure, there may have been people who have achieved a lot even while being physically disabled, but why should he be one of them. He is not supposed to be like this. I know what kind of people you guys are. Instead of trying to revive his legs, you are here consoling us just so that you don't have to do anything. If you do not wish to or are not capable enough to keep your patients absolutely fit and fine, then you shouldn't be a doctor." Raj exclaimed.

Seena understood his anger, but questioning her profession and capability as a doctor was wrong. "Mr. Malhotra, I understand your feelings, but raising a finger on my sincerity towards my profession and my patients is wrong. I am a surgeon because I am capable of being one. Rohit is healthy. He should even be discharged in a few days. As for his ability to walk, I have already said that there is no need to completely lose hope. I request you to pay attention to the positive side of things rather than the negative. It would help you and your family a lot. Please be in your senses that this is a hospital, not your office, you can't just falsely accuse me of not being faithful to my duties and not expect me to answer back. I am not your employee; I am a doctor who just saved your brother's life. Please respect that." She gave an assuring glance toward his parents and left.

4
SUSPICIONS

Raj was left speechless. No one had ever dared to talk back to him. He was angry, but also impressed that she had the courage to talk to him like that. He looked at his parents, who had been watching the argument, and sighed. "At least he is fine now." he shrugged. He then looked at the other doctor who was with Seena. "Can we meet him now?" The doctor asked them to wait for a few minutes and let him shift Rohit into a room. Soon, he called Raj to meet his brother. Raj nodded and went inside. By now Rohit had gained consciousness. As he entered the room, Raj saw a man, almost six feet tall, with brown hair, a fit body and a good- looking face, all covered in tubes, oxygen mask, tapes, etc.

"Rohit?"

"Raj?"

"Yes, it's me, Raj. How are you feeling now? Are you alright?"

"I am better and alive, I guess. Thanks to the doctor who did my operation."

Raj remembered his argument with Seena but didn't mention it to Rohit.

"Where are mom and dad?", Rohit asked.

" They are outside. I'll send them in when I go out."

Rohit nodded. There was complete silence in the room for a minute.

"So my legs are as good as dead now, aren't they?" Rohit said, breaking the silence.

Raj's head snapped towards him. "You know?", he asked, his voice almost a whisper.

Rohit looked at his brother, " Of course I do. The doctor told me. It's my body, I have to know." Raj sighed and nodded.

"You know what, I was obviously pretty upset upon hearing that I'll probably never walk again, but the doctor, the lady who saved my life, you know she encouraged me, gave me examples of disabled yet extremely successful people like Franklin D Roosevelt or Stephen Hawking and honestly, I feel like I am ready for anything. Roosevelt led a world war and Hawking researched and talked about black holes. I don't have to do anything like that, I just have to live a normal and peaceful life. Nothing too serious. So, I am chill."

Raj smiled at his brother's calm and confident personality. He also realized that Seena was right. She had come to make him understand her point, which was absolutely valid. And he had angrily burst upon her.

"Okay, I'll go now and send mom and dad in. Bye and take care."

Rohit smiled at his brother's love for him. Raj went out of the room, and asked his parents to go in. They went to meet their son and talked to him, comforted him and spent time with him.

Two days later, Raj received a call from the police station. After meeting Rohit, Raj and his parents had gone home, assured that Rohit was fine and improving. Now

Kehan was calling him to inform him that the owner of the runaway jeep had been identified and it was none other than the person who saved Rohit's life, Dr. Seena Khurrana. Raj was shocked to the core. He had started feeling a bit guilty about shouting on Seena for no reason, but this changed everything. She was the one who tried to kill Rohit, and then saved him later? Why? Kehan told him that Seena was being brought in for questioning and that he would inform Raj about the results of the investigation soon. Raj agreed and cut the call. He started thinking about she supposedly attacked his brother and then saved his life, but why? What was the point? He was unable to understand. If Seena wanted, she could have let him die, sure he and his family would have been upset and probably furious, but no one would be able to blame her. And if she didn't want to kill Rohit, and only injure him for the rest of his life, then why encourage him? He was lost in his thoughts and forgot all about the pending work that he had to finish.

Seena was brought in for questioning. The Lieutenant had arrested her from her home. She now sat on a chair, placed in the middle of a dark room with Param sitting in front of her, and an assistant inspector, standing in the corner taking notes.

So, Dr. Seena, we have confirmed that the jeep that tried to kill Mr. Rohit Malhotra, was on your name." The questioning began.

"I don't even own a jeep."

"Well, the facts and the number plate on the jeep say something else."

"Well, the facts are wrong and as for the number plate, I don't even own a jeep. I just have a car that is not working and has gone for repairs for the past 4 days. For all I know, someone could have stolen my number plate and put it on their jeep."

"Don't you think that's a bit farfetched?"

"Don't you think it would make absolutely no sense, if someone tries to kill a person and later on saves that very person's life?"

"And why would anyone specifically select your car for stealing the number plate?"

"I don't know, it was probably just a coincidence."

Param looked at her, straight in the eyes. He spoke after a minute or two,

"Give me the garage's number."

Seena gave it to him. He asked Kehan to call the garage and confirm if Seena's car was there and if it had the number plate on it or not. Kehan went out of the questioning room and did as he was told. He came back five minutes later.

"Sir, the owner of the garage confirmed that Miss Seena's car is indeed in the garage, but its number plate is missing. However, he doesn't have any idea where the license plate is or since when it's been missing. He said that only the mechanic who worked on the car could help us and at the moment he is unreachable. He is out of town and will be returning the day after tomorrow."

Param nodded and turned towards Seena.

"Doctor Seena, you are on house arrest for the next two days. You will not leave your home till the time you are proven innocent. You will not be going to the hospital either. Your phone will be with us. Do not even try to flee the country, and before leaving, give up all your cards and money. All your credit and debit cards and all accounts will be temporarily blocked. All your essentials that you require will be provided to you by us.

I would suggest you pray that the mechanic proves your innocence. Seena agreed to everything and went home with the escort. When she opened the door to her house, she saw a girl sitting, waiting for her. She was a pretty girl with average height. She had short hair with some freckles. Seena immediately recognized the girl as her colleague cum best friend, Krutika.

5

IS HE THE SAME ROHIT?

The police escort saw this too and took out her gun, thinking that Krutika was a thief. Before she could do anything, Seena said, " Wait! She is my colleague as well as my best friend. I know I am not supposed to meet anyone and if you want you can come in and stand beside me while we talk. I promise it won't take long either." The escort agreed and Seena went to Krutika who was surprised to see the police escort. Seena and Krutika sat on the couch with the police escort standing right behind them.

"What is happening? Why is she here? Where were you? I was calling you for so long, but you were not picking up. So, I came here to check up on you, but you were nowhere to be found." Krutika said it all in one breath. Seena sighed. She took a deep breath and explained everything to her friend, from the time Rohit came in her hospital as a patient to the point when she was taken in for questioning and was ordered house arrest. Krutika listened to her, carefully and patiently, not missing out on a single word. When Seena finished,

Krutika immediately asked,

"Okay, I understood. Don't worry, I know you are innocent. Nothing will happen. Also, can you tell me one thing, what did you say was the name of your patient?"

Seena looked at her as she was surprised at the question, but replied anyway, " Rohit Malhotra, why?" Krutika took out her phone from her purse and showed Seena a photo.

Seena's eyes widened. " Yes, this is him, but how do you..." Seena started to ask but trailed off as the realization hit her. " No way, he is not, is he?"

Krutika nodded excitedly.

"He is the same Rohit from college. How? The Rohit I knew was chubby and round, but this man is so handsome, and fit." Seena was shocked and confused.

"You lost touch with him after college, but I didn't, remember? Every time I tried to get you two to talk to each other, one of you became busy at the last moment. So, you both never saw each other after college and therefore you didn't recognize him when he came in your hospital." Krutika explained.

"Good thing I didn't too, because he was on the verge of dying and it would have been very difficult for me to operate upon him if I knew he was my friend."

Suddenly Seena looked at Krutika, "Kru, I don't know how to tell you this, but you do realize that Rohit may never be able to walk again, right? I know you love him, and nothing can change that but since you will be his wife in the future, you will have to help him in a lot of tasks."

Krutika had actually forgotten about it in the excitement of having a chance to see Rohit again. She went silent. She closed her eyes and realized that Seena was saying the truth. The fact that Rohit was physically disabled didn't change her love for him and that's all that mattered to her. She smiled and opened her eyes, only to find Seena smiling back at her. She had understood her friend's thoughts by her smile. Seena looked at the escort, still standing behind them and asked Krutika to leave for the time being and refrain from reminding Rohit about their friendship as she wanted to give him a surprise after being proven innocent. Krutika agreed and left. On the other hand, Raj was also thinking about Rohit's love life. He thought about the reaction of the girl Rohit had loved since college and if she would accept him anymore. He hoped so.

Everything went normally. Seena was at her home with the police escort. Rohit's family came to visit him. The investigation was also going on. Param had decided to check the footage of the CCTV cameras near the garage and ask people if they had seen Seena come there. Everyone denied seeing her. Param was almost sure by now that Seena was innocent but had to wait for the mechanic to confirm about the number plate. It was Monday, the day he was supposed to return. As soon as he reached the garage, the owner of the garage asked him to report to the police station and give his statement as ordered by the Lieutenant. The mechanic agreed and confirmed to Param that the license plate was present when the car first came in. All doubts of Seena's involvement in the case were removed. Param ordered Kehan to call the police escort and tell her to bring Seena to the police station so that she could pick up her things.

"Also, ask the banks to unblock all her accounts and cards." Kehan nodded. He informed the escort of what to do and called the banks and got all of Seena's accounts unblocked. Finally, he called Raj and told him about the progress in the case. As soon as he cut the call, Raj sighed heavily. He was happy to know that the only girl who had the guts to stand up to him was not a criminal. Seena came and collected her possessions, told Krutika the good news and then decided to surprise Rohit that evening.

6

REUNITED

Krutika was really nervous as well as excited. She was thinking of Rohit's reaction, if he would be happy to see them again. She was sure he would. She kept thinking about their surprise all day long. Finally, in the evening they went to meet Rohit. Seena had a smile on her lips while Krutika's excitement was clear from her face. They reached the hospital and entered. They saw Raj and his parents discussing something. When Raj's mother saw Seena, she beckoned her to come over. The two girls went towards her.

"Dr. Seena, I am so sorry. You had to face so much trouble for my son's case. I mean you saved his life, and still they doubted you. That was uncalled for. Honestly, I am really sorry on behalf of the police. We have already told them our opinion on their way of handling this case. Once again, I am so so sor.." Mrs. Malhotra was apologizing when Seena interrupted her. " It's absolutely fine Mrs. Malhotra. You do not need to apologize for anything. As for the police, they were just doing their job. And anyway, I have been proven innocent right, so no worries." Seena assured her. Mrs. Malhotra smiled at Seena, and she smiled back.

"Dr. Seena, you saved my son's life, you are like my daughter now, please don't call me Mrs. Malhotra. You can call me Riyalli Aunty or just aunty instead."

"Then that applies to you too. Please stop calling me Dr, Seena and just call me Seena or whatever you want." Seena requested with a cute smile. Riyalli nodded. Seena looked at Krutika who was looking nervous. She understood what was going on in her mind. She put an arm around Krutika's shoulder and whispered, "You can do it Kruts, they are his family and if you want to meet him, you must at least inform them first and tell them that you two know each other. Don't worry you don't need to tell her that you are his girlfriend." She winked. Krutika was dumbfounded. She quickly recovered from her original shock at Seena's teasing and spoke,

"Umm...Aunty? If I can call you that" Riyalli nodded and Krutika continued, " My name is Krutika. Actually, Rohit and I know each other from college. We were best friends and till date we have kept in touch. Seena was also part of our group. Basically, Seena and I wanted to surprise Rohit by telling him that we are his friends. Can we?" Mrs. Malhotra looked at Seena for confirmation who nodded confirming Krutika's statement. She then smiled at the two doctors and happily gave them permission. The two girls thanked her and went towards Rohit's room. When they were just outside the door and were about to go in, Krutika stopped. Seena, who immediately noticed this, stopped too and raised her brows in confusion, seeing which Krutika hastened to explain,

"I am just very nervous. Will he remember me? I mean of course he will, we have kept in touch all these years, but still. What will be his reaction? He is already admitted in the hospital and is suffering so much. He just lost his legs, he isn't well, will it be right to give him such a shocking news at this time?" Krutika kept blabbering.

" Ssshh.. Kru, stop worrying for no reason. His reaction will be epic. He will be so happy, you know him. And as for him losing his legs and suffering and being in the hospital, then in that case he needs you even more right now. He needs assurance that you are by his side, no matter what. He needs your support. He is already upset, understandably, and at this time what could be better than surprising him and bringing a smile on his face." Seena calmed her friend down.

Krutika took a deep breath and nodded at Seena, indicating that she had understood and was ready to go in. Seena smiled at her, and they went inside. They saw Rohit looking at nothing in particular and thinking something. Seena looked at Krutika assuring her and went towards Rohit.

"Hey"

Rohit came out of his thoughts and looked at Seena.

" Hey"

" How are you feeling? Better?"

"I guess. I mean I can't really be better because I am sure I cannot grow my legs back. Right?" Seena and Krutika chuckled. Rohit, who hadn't yet noticed Krutika's presence, looked at her after hearing her voice and was astounded. The two got lost in each other's eyes.

Seena observed this and fake coughed, bringing the two back from their dreamland. They blushed. Rohit was still perplexed and was about to say something but before he could, Seena explained,

"So Rohit, she is my bestie, Krutika Sharma, about to be Malhotra." She winked at him.

His eyes widened. "How...?"

"Rohit, she is Seena, from college, remember?" Krutika said.

"No, no. How will he remember? He will only remember his girlfriend, why will he care for his best friend." Seena tried to sound dramatic.

Rohit blushed, but quickly hid it and objected," Seena, you are my angel, how could I possibly forget you."

"Yeah, and Kruts is your queenie, Mr. Devil." Seena couldn't stop her teasing and Rohit and Krutika couldn't stop blushing.

7
DEVIL, QUEENIE AND ANGEL

Suddenly, Mr. Malhotra entered the room, along with his wife and Raj.

"Angel, Queenie? What is all this? Rohit? Seena? Krutika?" Riyalli asked.

"Actually, aunty I think it would be better if your son explains about Angel and Queenie." Krutika said pointing towards Rohit. Everyone looked at Rohit and he sighed. After giving a glare to Krutika which went unnoticed by everyone except her, he explained,

"Mom, Dad, she is Kruts or Krutika and you all already know Seena. Well, we three have known each other since college. And as for Angel and Queenie, I used to call Seenu angel and Kruts Queenie in college, and they called me Devil."

Raj suddenly thought of something.

"Rohit, is she the same girl?" Rohit became a bit shy but nodded. Raj smiled and went towards his brother and hugged him. "Congrats bro." Everyone was confused except Raj and Rohit. "What is happening? And fine these are your nicknames for each other but why these nicknames and what are you congratulating Rohit for?" Mr. Malhotra asked.

Seena suddenly understood everything and spoke up, "I think I know what the congratulations was for, but before that let me answer your question, sir. We call Rohit Devil because during college he saved us from bullies and was like a real devil to them. So that's why. And he calls me Angel, because I used to love to help people a lot. So, I guess I was like an angel, and he started calling me that. And finally, the reason behind him addressing Kruts here as Queenie, well, I think it would be better if he himself told you that."

Mr. Malhotra turned to look at his son who was starting to get nervous. "No need to be nervous, bro. Just say it." Raj prompted.

Rohit took a deep breath, looked at Raj and Seena and then at Krutika who was smiling at him, indicating that she was always beside him, no matter what. He finally looked at his parents and announced, "I call Kru Queenie because...because I love her. And she loves me too. And Raj knew that I loved a girl and he had heard me call her Queenie sometimes. So, when he heard me calling her by the same nickname as the one, I had for the girl I loved, he understood that it's the same girl and congratulated me on meeting her as we weren't able to meet after college. We kept in touch, but we never actually met."

There was complete silence in the room. No one spoke a word for a few minutes. Mr. and Mrs. Malhotra were shocked and were trying to digest the fact that their son had a girlfriend. Suddenly, Riyalli smiled and said, "I must say you have a pretty good choice, Rohit. Learn something from him Raj. Krutika, you are indeed a very beautiful girl. I am surprised that you love him."

Everyone chuckled except Raj and Rohit. "Mom", they said in unison.

"Okay, now leave all this. And Krutika, do you know about...?" Mr. Malhotra started speaking but trailed off. However, Krutika understood what he was saying and replied, " Yes, I know uncle, but I don't care. I love his heart, his soul, his personality, and that hasn't changed, so I have no problem." Everyone smiled at her. "Well then, let me make a formal introduction, my name is Rehan Malhotra, I am a well-known businessman, but I have retired now my older son Raj is the current CEO of our company. You have already met my wife, Riyalli Malhotra and I think that you already know everything about Rohit." Rohit's father teased.

Krutika blushed and nodded. "I am Krutika, Krutika Sharma. I am a dentist by profession. She is my best friend cum sister, Seena Khurrana, a reputed surgeon. And that's all." Rehan was impressed and nodded. "Ok then, the four of you chat, and we will go back home I think.", he said looking at his wife to confirm. Riyalli agreed and he continued speaking, "Also, Seena, you call Riyalli aunty, right? So, you can call me uncle too. And Krutika you should also call us uncle and aunty, at least for now."

" Yes, uncle." Seena and Krutika said at the same time. They were both feeling very touched. Mr. and Mrs. Malhotra left.

"So, Rohit won't you tell me about your college and how you met my to be sister-in-law?" Raj teased. Krutika and Rohit blushed.

"Fine, I will tell. So, we three were in the same year. Angel and Queenie were already friends from before, as they were roommates. Queenie and I had most of our classes together, but barely knew each other. One day, I saw some boy proposing to her in the college garden. She rejected his proposal, but he didn't accept the rejection and started threatening her. It was already evening and was getting pretty dark, so I was not able to see the boy's face. He even started going near her and touching her in inappropriate places. She was really scared. She was shouting for Angel, but Angel was not there. I saw this and obviously how could I see a boy misbehaving with a girl and sitting quietly. I went towards them and beat the boy till he started calling Queenie as sister and ran away. Queenie thanked me, and we started talking. She made me meet Angel. We three became friends. And ultimately, I developed a crush on Krutika. I was scared to confess, so I talked about it to Angel as she was like my sister and Queenie's best friend. Turns out Queenie had also developed a crush on me and told Angel about it because again she was like my sister and her best friend. However, Angel could not tell me that Queenie had a crush on me, and she could not tell Queenie that I had a crush on her because we both had made her promise to keep it a secret. So, what she did was that she planned to get us together. One evening, she asked us to play truth and dare and we agreed. I chose truth, and she asked me whom did I had a crush on, if I did. Now, I was tongue tied, I mean how could I take my crush's name in front of my crush. I said that I didn't want to answer the question and that I chose to dare. So, she gave me a dare to perform a song chosen by her, in front of the whole college and that I had to do the very next day. I agreed. She gave me Queenie's favorite song. I was not much of a singer, but I liked playing the guitar and I liked to hum to songs, so I thought that why not. I performed. After the performance, Queenie came running to me and hugged me. At first, I was shocked, but then I hugged her back. She told me that the song I had performed was her all-time favorite, but she hadn't heard it for a long time because she was so busy in her studies, that she had stopped listening to songs. I was honestly surprised. I wasn't expecting the song to be her favorite and her to be so touched by it, but I think when I saw how happy and impressed, she was with me and when she hugged me, I got the courage to propose to her. So that's what I did. Actually, I didn't do it, Angel made me do it. In the evening, she asked me and Queenie to meet her in her room. We went, but she wasn't there. The room was beautifully decorated with Queenie and I's pictures and a romantic song was playing. As I said, I was already planning to propose to her, so I went to the center of the room and confessed my love. She said yes and we became a couple. All thanks to my Angel." All of them smiled.

8
MEMORIES

"I didn't know that besides being a doctor, you were also a matchmaker." Raj said to Seena.

"Oh well, I am a lot more things than just a doctor and matchmaker. Don't worry, you just met me but with time, if I wish, you can get to know me even better." Seena replied with attitude.

"I agree with her. Raj you wouldn't believe but she is a very mysterious girl. Like in college, at first she used to be a very sweet and innocent type girl but one day when a boy proposed to her in front of the whole college, she became savage as hell." Rohit spoke.

"Oh, come on Rohit, you know very well, that I did not become savage for no reason. He was literally showing me attitude while proposing to me. Well, if he was so full of himself then I was no less either." Seena said, defending herself.

"I know, I know but let me at least tell him that what had exactly happened. So, it was in the second year of college that this happened. It was break, the three of us were going to the cafeteria. We used to meet up after our classes and go together. So, as we were walking, while chatting about studies and other things, a boy named

Pankit came to Angel. He was her partner in one of her classes, I think, and he thought that Angel liked him. So, he came, sat down on one knee, and said, 'Seena, will you be my girlfriend. I really like you.' " Rohit mimicked the boy and continued, "Before she or any of us could say anything, he got up from his knees and said 'I know you also love me and want to be my girlfriend. So just say yes and set yourself for life.' And as you can probably guess, she gave him a savage answer and rejected him."

"Ok, but what did she say?" Raj asked.

"That she will only tell." Rohit announced.

"Fine, I will. So, I just simply said that I was going to answer him sweetly and politely which I was but because of his attitude, I was not going to do that anymore. So, I just asked him if he slept too much so that he was able to see me as his girlfriend in his dreams because it is not possible in reality. I told him to wait for a few years and when he misunderstood me and asked if I am asking him to wait to make me his girlfriend, I replied that he should wait for me or some other doctors to find out a cure for his level of attitude and misunderstanding so that he can be treated." All of them laughed.

"I bet he ran away after facing that kind of embarrassment. " Raj confirmed.

"He did. And after he ran away, we along with the rest of the students that were present there, were shocked. We never expected her to be like that. We always thought of her as a simple and sweet person, but we were proven wrong. Since then, her level of savageness never decreased. Though, she is nice and sweet too, most of the time but, when need be, she can make anyone speechless with her savage words." Krutika also joined the conversation.

"Now that you have told him about me, it is my turn to tell him about you two. You know Raj, Rohit did used to save us from bullies, sure, and he had saved Kru also from that boy, and that is why we started calling him devil. However, one time after these two became a couple, Rohit got jealous of a boy. Actually, what happened was that Kru and a boy were project partners in one of her classes. They both shared a brother and sister type bond. So, one day, when they were coming out of the class they shared a hug, just a small brotherly - sisterly hug. Rohit had been waiting for Kru to come out and when he saw her hug the boy, he got super jealous and left from there. He didn't even talk to Kru for two whole days. She always used to ask me if she did anything wrong, that why was he behaving like that, and I had no idea either. During this time Kru was also spending time with that boy because of the project they had. And that made Rohit even more jealous. So, on the night of the second day, he went to that boy's room and punched him in the face. And I guess that boy was probably a pretty deep sleeper because he didn't even wake up from the punch. The next morning when he did wake up, he was surprised to see his face a bit red and his cheek a bit swollen. During break, when he came into the cafeteria, Kru saw him and immediately to him because she saw him as her brother and if her brother were hurt, she would go to him, right? Anyway, so she went to him and asked him about his injury. Rohit saw this and got even more jealous. As I was also present there, I noticed his reaction and by connecting the dots, I understood that he was the one who had punched the boy because of jealousy. By then Kru had taken that boy to the clinic and honestly Rohit's facial expression was so funny. That evening, when Kru and I were in my room, chatting about random things, after taking a break from studies. That time, I told her about Rohit being the one who punched that boy and the reason behind it. She quickly stood up and went to Devil's room, held him by the collar of his shirt and pulled him to our room. When they both came, I saw that he was so scared, like I had never seen him that afraid. I could barely control my laughter. Kru asked me to hand her some pillows and I did, and she started hitting Devil with them. He was trying to save himself, but her aim was too good. He kept asking her that what had he done but she was busy in beating him. So, with a lot of difficulty, I suppressed my urge to laugh and told him the reason. I also told him that Kruts and that boy had a bro-sis type relation and that he didn't have to be jealous. He was shocked and started apologizing but Kruts was not listening. She finally stopped after a few more minutes and started scolding Rohit for being jealous without any reason. And that was it for me. I started laughing so bad, but they didn't care. They were busy in their argument. I quietly left the room with some of my books and went to Kruts room to study. After about an hour or so, I went back to my room and saw Kruts sitting on the bed while Rohit was sitting on the floor, still apologizing. I was quite irritated by now and just wanted some peace, so I made them sort things out. I somehow convinced Kru to forgive him, and she did and everything was normal except Kru asked Devil to say sorry to that boy also. Devil, having no choice, agreed and immediately went and said sorry to him. That boy was also a good person and forgave him. Although, I still cannot forget how scared he looked when he was being beaten ruthlessly by the pillows and Kruts." Seena finished telling the memory and laughed along with Raj while Rohit and Krutika were feeling embarrassed. "

"Wow, I had no idea that my brother who is a tiger in front of everyone becomes a scaredy cat in front of his future wife." Raj teased Rohit. "By the way, that was his story, isn't there any story for Krutika?", he asked.

"Now you have said the right thing. Of course, there is a story for her also." Rohit admitted.

"Then tell"

" Ok. So, the thing is that Queenie was always a fan of sports. She was amazing at a lot of things like football, tennis, badminton, etc. Everyone knew that. However, this one time there was a basketball match between the girls and the boys. Now, the thing was that, for the first half of the game, it was a tie most of the time. However, while scoring the last basket before the intermission, the star player of the girls' team got injured. She was the one making all the baskets and now had twisted her hand while throwing the ball. After the break, that girl still kept playing but she did not try to do any baskets anymore. One of the other girls tried to score the baskets instead of her but she wasn't as good as the first one. She wasn't bad, she was also playing pretty nicely, just the first one had played better. By the time there were only 10 minutes left for the match the boys' team was leading by 7 points. Just at that moment, Queenie came and said that she would also play. She is not very tall, as you can see, she is pretty much average height, and it was the same that time also. So many people had doubts about her game." Rohit started recounting the story.

"Yes, and in fact even the both of us were doubting her for this one because we had never seen her play basketball before. Anyway, she came and entered the game as a replacement for the girl who had injured her wrist. She had to play as the team captain and star scorer. No one was ready to give her that role, but she was so confident that they gave up and hesitantly gave her the position. What happened next was unbelievable. With the help of her team, Kruts scored basket after basket. She was literally scoring a basket every minute. The girls on the team were amazing at defending and now that they could focus on that, since they had Kru to score the baskets, the boys were not able to score any points. There were thirty seconds left, when the score became tied. The ball was with Kru. Two or three of the boys started to round her up to stop her from scoring. They were standing in between her and the basket. So, Kru did a backflip and then threw the ball over the boys' heads and guess what? The ball went straight through the basket with ten seconds still left. The boys caught the ball and tried to score one last point but with the girls defending they failed, and the time was up. Kru made the girls win. She did not have a great height, but she was very flexible and had really good aim. From that day onwards, no one ever doubted her abilities for anything, including us." Seena continued and ended the story.

"This was also after we started dating, by the way.", Krutika said, shy.

9
SHADOW

Awesome, you know, I also love to play basketball, maybe someday we both can play together Krutika." Raj playfully suggested.

"Sure."

"Anyways guys, I have some work, so I will be going. And Raj, didn't you have something to do too?" Seena said, indicating to Raj with her eyes that she wanted to let the couple spend some time alone. Raj, who was confused at first and was about to say that he did not have any work, understood her meaning, when he saw her looking at his brother and Krutika. He nodded and said,

"Yes, thanks for reminding. I will also come with you." Seena and Raj left the room. Outside, they stopped by the water cooler.

"Umm, I wanted to say something", Raj suddenly spoke.

"Hmm", Seena hummed while filling up her glass with water.

"Actually, I wanted to say that...I am sorry, I did not completely believe you at first. I mean all the evidence was against you. I was confused that why would you save him, if you wanted to kill him? I am really sorry."

"Raj, I don't know you that well, but I can guarantee that I know Rohit extremely well, and that he is like my brother. I can never hurt him. And I don't blame you for not trusting me that much. We are pretty much strangers. The only connection between us is your brother. So, I can understand your point of view. He is your little brother, your life, if there were any doubt on anyone hurting him, you would be angry, but the fact that you did not let your feelings overpower your stability of mind, you knew that I couldn't do it, you were confused, that fact is very impressive and worth praising. Don't worry, you did not hurt me in any way."

"Thank you."

Seena nodded. "Now that we know that I was not the culprit and also Rohit is better and has Kruts to take care of him, I have a suggestion. I don't know how long it is going to take the police to find out the real criminal. So, why don't you and I team up and find out the mastermind behind all of this, together? As friends?" Seena suggested.

"Fine with me. I am ready for it. I also want to know who caused my brother to be in this condition."

They both smiled at each other.

"Great, then why waste time? Why don't we go into my cabin and discuss our plan of action? Ok?"

"Ok."

They went to her cabin and Raj sat down on the couch while Seena sat on her chair. After thinking in silence for a few minutes, Seena spoke, "I think we should start from the start. Firstly, what we know is that someone in a jeep pushed your brother's bike, due to which all this happened. The jeep driver had stolen my car's number plate, when I had given my car in for repair, which may or may not mean that the driver knew about the garage and probably gave had his jeep serviced there only. If we can talk to the owner of the garage or even one of the employees, then we can find out if the jeep is actually serviced there and if our suspicions are correct. And if they are, then in that case we should be able to find the jeep's real number plate, have it tracked down and reach the jeep driver. However, there is an issue."

"What issue? The idea seems perfectly fine to me. Except for the fact that we cannot be absolutely sure yet whether the jeep does go there or not."

"Of course, that is there, but there is one more problem. I have a gut feeling that this is not as simple as it seems. I don't think that a random person would plan something like this without reason. There has to be someone else behind all this, but the question is who?"

"I guess you are right. Well, for the time being we have no idea who the culprit is, but we can start by going with your plan and talking to the owner and the employees of the garage. It will be a start and maybe this way we can slowly catch the real culprit too."

"Hmm. Ok then. I will call and fix a meeting with the owner tomorrow. If he is not able to help us, then we can go there and question the workers."

"Ok, let's do that."

"Yes. By the way I wanted to ask you something, if you don't mind."

"I don't. Go ahead."

"Where were you when Rohit was in college? I mean you both are almost the same age, but I never saw you. How? I mean Rohit had told us that he had a brother but nothing else. We didn't even know your name."

Raj chuckled a bit, before speaking, "Actually, I was studying in London. As I am two years older than him,

I finished school first and went to London to study business. Rohit was also going to come but he didn't because he did not want to leave our parents alone. Our parents work really hard. They share the household chores and also work on company matters. They both are very busy most of the time. So, Rohit decided to stay back and help them. As for me, I rarely came here. I was there only, doing internships, studying and all that. I also wanted to become a lawyer, so I studied law too. I spent a few years there completing my studies in both professions. When I came back, I joined the company and our parents retired. Rohit had already been helping out our dad, so he was already a part of the business and continued acting as president, the post just below the CEO, but it is just for namesake. His primary focus is on being an advocate. He only helps out when need be. Now, I needed him and when I asked him to take over the position of manager of one of our biggest factories, this happened."

"Oh, then it must have cost you a lot, right? I mean after his accident; he has been here only. So, hasn't your company suffered any loss? I mean you must have a time limit to finish your orders, right? I am sure the workers would do their job but there needs to be a supervisor to ensure that the work is done effectively and efficiently. Also, don't be surprised if I know about business, I have done business studies too, alongside medical. So, I know about it. And yeah, as far as I know, Devil was also studying to become a lawyer."

"He must have. He was always interested in law. Like whenever we talked on the phone, he would never forget to ask me about my law studies. So, I am not surprised. And as for my company, well, it cannot be helped. I had fired the previous supervisor and I have no one to take care of it. Honestly, after knowing that you have done business studies, and are my friend too now, I would have asked you to take care of it, but you are also already so busy with your surgeries and other things. Plus, we have to find the person behind Rohit's accident too, so I don't want to put too much pressure on you. I think I will only try to handle the factory somehow."

"Hey, chill out. Sure, I am busy, but so are you. You are the CEO of the company after all. And even you are helping in finding the culprit. No need to stress yourself so much. I will help you in handling the factory. Sure, I won't be able to handle it all the time, but we can do it together, right? I mean when I am free, I can do it and when I am not free, you can. Or even Kruts can help, I think. I know she told me once that her relative is a businessman, so she knows how to handle it well. And also, she was there with me in my business studies course too. So, she can also help out. I am sure she would love to." Seena assured him.

He smiled at her and nodded. "Thanks a lot. You have relieved me of such a big tension."

"That's what friends are for."

"Well, I think I will take my leave now. Bye and thanks for your help once again."

"Bye and no need of thanks. I have to help my Devil and Shadow." Seena said with a smile.

"Shadow? Who is shadow?"

"You"

"Me? Why?"

"Well, the way you apologized to me, and the fact that we are going to handle the factory and Devil's mystery together, why not give you a nickname. Plus, we are friends and we both like to tease Devil and Kruts, so you are like my partner. So yeah"

"Then I should also give you a nickname"

" You don't need to. I already have one, Angel. You can call me that only."

"Ok then, I will. And I will also call Rohit as Devil and Krutika by Kruts. Fine? You can include me in your gang."

"You are included. Since I am the eldest in my gang because I am a year older than the other two, I declare you as part of the group."

"Thanks, and now I am the eldest in the group as you are also one year younger to me."

"Well not exactly a year, I would say few months, but ok.", she smiled at him. Raj also smiled back. "Should we keep a name for the mystery?" Seena asked.

"Sure, but what?"

"How about Devil's Mission?"

"I like it. Good choice."

"Thanks." Raj then bid bye to Seena and left.

10

MISSION DEVIL

After he left, Seena called the garage owner and fixed the meeting. The next day Seena and Raj went to meet him. He was slightly plump with a bright smile on his round face. "Hello Mr. Surash, this is my friend Raj. You already know the whole story since the police must have told you but let me recount it for you. I had given my car to you for servicing but apparently someone stole the number plate from my car, put it on his or her jeep and then attempted to kill one of my close friends with that jeep. Also, the victim is Raj's brother." Seena explained the whole story.

"I do not know how it happened. We are usually very careful with who can enter our working area. After talking to you on the phone yesterday, I asked my employees about the same but neither of them knew anything. I am also shocked to know about this mistake on our part and I deeply apologize for the same. If I can help you in any way, please tell me." Surash replied.

" Do you have CCTV cameras here?" Raj suddenly asked.

"Yes, we do"

"Can we please check the footage? I know the police must have seen it already, but I also want to check it once in case they missed out anything." Raj said.

Surash agreed and showed them the footage. While Raj was watching the video, Seena was looking at the time frame. In the middle of the tape, she saw something suspicious. She asked Surash to rewind the tape by a few seconds and play it again after zooming on the time frame. He did so and soon everyone realized that the footage had been tampered with. The video was going smoothly but a part of the tape was missing. There was no footage of the time period between 1 AM and 1:30 AM, two days before the accident. The video had been edited so smoothly that unless you specifically focus on the time frame you wouldn't be able to catch the mistake. Seena had an idea that if the number plate can be stolen then the video can be edited too. Hence, she was focusing on the time frame and her doubts were confirmed. Raj and Seena thanked Surash for his help and left the garage. Once they were outside, Seena said, "Raj, I have an idea. Why don't we ask around if anyone saw anything yesterday. Maybe someone could have heard or seen something that night."

"I guess it would cause no harm. So why not? Sure, let's go. You go towards the right, and I will go left."

Seena agreed and they both left. They went up to people and questioned them. After half an hour they both met near the place where their car was parked. "I didn't find anything." Raj confessed.

"I did. An old couple saw a jeep parked there, one night. It was the same night as the missing footage. The description of the jeep was exactly the same as the description of the one that caused the accident. They were suspicious of the jeep since it was late at night and the garage was closed. Therefore, they copied the number of the jeep in case something happened. Now I have the number of the plate."

"That's amazing. You are really lucky today. I mean you found the fault in the CCTV footage and now you got the actual plate number of the jeep. By the way, don't the police know about this?"

"No, I don't think they do because the police came here a few days ago, and this couple had gone out of town somewhere and had just returned when I met them."

"Oh ok"

"And about me being lucky, it's probably just a coincidence, but I won't mind being actually lucky."

They both chuckled. Seena called Krutika and told her about the plan and the progress they had made. She asked Krutika to have the jeep tracked. Krutika had many connections and Seena knew that she would be able to do it. Krutika found out the location of the jeep and told Seena, who told Raj. Raj and Seena drove to the place and found the jeep.

"The jeep is here but where is the driver?" Raj asked.

"No idea, but listen, if we just straight up confront the driver, then he is going to simply deny everything. I know we have witnesses, but we don't have any real proof. So, instead, we should try to get him talking and then surprise him." Seena suggested.

"That way he would be taken aback, and we would be able to catch him and make him confess. I think we should also record our conversation, for proof."

"Yes, that's a good idea. By the way, you have started understanding me very much. Are you like stalking me or something, because I don't see any other way you would understand my plans."

"Oh really? Don't you think that I have a brain of my own to understand things?"

"I am sure you do, but I am not sure if the owner of that brain is capable enough to understand my brain."

"You... listen, I am not a stalker, and this is not the time to argue."

"I know, I know, I just thought that the atmosphere was getting too serious for our own health and decided to have some fun with you. However, now let's focus." Seena first chuckled and then immediately turned serious. Raj was shocked at her ability to change her personality so easily. They both went to find the driver of the jeep. They found a man standing in the shade of a tree, near the jeep and went up to him. He was an average heighted man, with a light beard and dressed in a simple shirt and pant.

"Excuse me, we are reporters, and we are surveying jeep drivers about their lives. Since most people in this country are living in poverty, we want to find out the problems faced by different people in living their daily life so that we can bring it to light in front of the government. I was hoping that you would be able to help us." Seena made up a fake story and told the man.

"Sure, ask what you want. I am a jeep driver myself."

"Oh, that's great. Do you mind showing us your jeep? It can help us understand your daily routine better." Raj asked.

"Why not? The jeep behind you is mine only. My name is Garhan."

Seena and Raj looked at each other. "Well, Mr. Garhan, can you please tell us something about your daily life?" Seena said.

"My daily life is pretty boring most of the time. Just transferring goods here and there. There are days when you don't have any work and then there are days that you have to travel very long distances and get tired. It's nothing special."

"I understand. Have you ever indulged in something that you may have regretted later on? Also, what is your relationship with the law like? I mean there is a lot of corruption, so have you faced any problems in that matter. Don't worry, it's just a survey and your story won't come out. It's going to remain anonymous. We may know your name, but we are not going to tell anyone." Raj spoke.

"Ok, you both don't look like you would really lie. I am not sure I regret anything, but I don't really have the best relations with the law. I mean I am fine most of the time and have no problems with the police but if you say that I am friendly with them or comfortable with them, then I am not."

"Of course, we understand you. You know something, a criminal can never have good relations with the police. Specially a person who can try to kill someone and have no regrets." Seena acclaimed. Garhan was taken aback, just as expected. Before he could say anything, Seena continued, "Such a person can have no problems with the police only because they haven't caught him yet. Once they do, he would never be at a lack of trouble with them." Seena smiled sarcastically.

"Who are you and what do you mean by trying to kill someone? I didn't kill anyone. I am not a criminal. So, watch what you are saying."

"Wait, wait, we never said that the person we are talking about is you. Then why did you just assume that we were talking about you?" Raj asked.

Garhan's eyes widened. He knew that he had been caught.

"Now, are you going to tell us that why did you try to kill Rohit? Or will we have to call the police and have them interrogate you? By the time they arrive I honestly don't know what we will do to you." Seena threatened him.

"No, no, I will tell you everything. I just did it for money. I was bored of this simple life and got tempted. I am really sorry."

" Who gave you the money?" Raj shouted.

"I don't know. I only know that it was someone from the Malhotra Industries and he just told me to follow the bike and kill him in an intentional accident. That's all."

"What?" Seena and Raj both shouted at the same time. They looked at each other. Seena took a deep breath and said, "Raj, we can discuss this later, but for now, let's hand him over to the authorities." Raj agreed and they took the jeep driver with them. After giving him to the police and explaining everything, they both went back to the hospital to meet Rohit and Krutika and tell them about what they had learnt.

11
DISCHARGED

They went inside Rohit's room and saw him looking bright and happy. Krutika was sitting beside him and had a similar expression on her face. Raj and Seena went towards them. "What happened guys? Why do you both look so happy and excited?" Seena asked.

"Actually, Rohit is getting discharged soon. That's why we are so happy." Krutika explained. Raj and Seena smiled and congratulated Rohit.

"Anyway, we also have good news. I found the jeep driver who tried to kill Rohit and now he is in prison." Raj announced.

"You mean we. Don't forget that you would have found nothing had it not been for me finding the mistake in the footage." Seena corrected him.

"Oh, come on, I am sure I would have found it by myself too. Also, if I hadn't suggested that we should record our conversation with that Garhan, we would have had no proof against him."

"I agree with you, and I never said that I did everything on my own because I didn't. However, you said that you were the one who got him caught, whereas I was also there with you, and I helped catch him. So don't forget that. There's no one here whom you can impress by taking all the credit yourself and showing that you are a brave and smart man, okay?"

"I am a brave and smart man."

"I never said you aren't. I just said that you don't need to show off. And don't you dare to forget to give me my credit ever again."

"Fine."

"Calm down both of you. Who is Garhan and will you both tell us what exactly happened?" Krutika interrupted their argument. Raj and Seena glared at each other and then explained the whole story.

"So, you mean to say that someone from our company is trying to kill me, right?" Rohit confirmed.

"Yes, but we don't know who." Raj admitted.

"One thing is for sure. This person must have a high post in your company. Otherwise, he wouldn't have been able to arrange for the money that he gave to Garhan." Seena acclaimed.

Krutika nodded and said, "Yes, that's true but what if we are wrong? What if it's no one from their company but from some other company? This mastermind may have lied to that jeep driver in order to ruin your company's reputation and complicate this whole matter."

"That is a possibility, but we still need to check our staff. We cannot take any risks." Raj replied. All of them discussed the mystery for a little longer before everyone left the room except Rohit. Outside the room, Seena asked, "Do you think it's right to involve Rohit in this? I mean his life could still be in danger and he must be stressed about his condition. Should we disturb him more?"

"Well, even if we don't involve him, the situation is not going to be any less dangerous. And it's not like we are asking him to help us or something, we are just keeping him informed, nothing else. That should not cause any trouble." Seena nodded and all of them left for their homes. After two days, Rohit got discharged and went home. He had to use a wheelchair since he was not able to walk. Seeing his state always made his family sad and increased Raj's motivation to find the real culprit. Both Seena and Raj were busy in these days and didn't have time to think about the mission. Raj was finally free and decided to visit Seena in her hospital. Once he reached it, he asked the receptionist about Seena's whereabouts. She told him that Seena was in her cabin. Raj thanked her and left for Seena's cabin. He knocked on the door and when he heard Seena ask him to come in, he went inside. Seena was checking one of her patient's files and looked up as she heard someone enter the room. She saw Raj and was surprised. "Raj? You here? What happened?"

"Ms. Angel, I think you have forgotten that we were solving a mystery."

"I haven't forgotten anything. I was just surprised to see you here. Anyway, you are right, we should focus on the case as much as possible so that Devil can be safe."

"Exactly. So, do you have any idea what we should do next? I have already run a check on all my employees, and I didn't find anything suspicious. I double checked everything just to make sure that I don't miss out on any details."

"Hmm, all we know is that someone from your company is betraying you but we don't know who is it."

"Yes."

Suddenly Seena remembered something. "Do you remember what Krits had said? That someone may be trying to frame your company. I think I know how we can find out if that's the case. Garhan told us that he had never seen the face of the person who planned all this, so, he would have probably been contacted by phone. I think the first thing to do is to check his call records and try to match them with the phone numbers of your employees and your own office phones. As far as I know there are no phone booths near your company. We should also confirm at what time the person called Garhan. If it was during the day, then we can find out if the person, the mastermind is really one of your employees or not."

"Good thinking, but how are we going to check the call records?"

"I am pretty sure I can get that done. You just collect the information about your employees and your office phones so that we can try and match. Ok?"

"Ok."

"How about we meet the day after tomorrow at your home and discuss the mystery further and match the numbers too. I can meet Rohit too and check up on him."

"Fine with me."

"Great, see you soon then."

"See you soon. Bye."

"Bye Shadow"

Raj smiled and left. Seena also got back to her work. The next day, Seena called someone for the call records and managed to get them. Raj also gathered all the necessary information about his employees. They both were eager to match their documents and find out the real culprit. Seena had thought of something else too which she decided to discuss with Raj and the others when she meets him. While Raj had also had an idea and wanted to discuss it with Seena and the others. Krutika had also been invited to the Malhotras' house. The following day, everyone met as planned and Raj and Seena tried to match the numbers. However, they failed. The calls had been made at night and the numbers didn't match any of the employees' phone numbers. They shared this news with Rohit and Krutika.

"Guys, even though this was a failed attempt, I had thought of something." Seena said.

"Me too, I had also had an idea." Raj added.

"Oh, ok, but let me say first. I have a feeling that the culprit is not from Rohit and Raj's company." Seena announced.

"Even I think so because why would the person say his company's name. That would just make it easier to catch him. It just doesn't make any sense." Raj reasoned.

"That was exactly what I had in mind. However, I would not like to eliminate any possibilities yet, even though it is highly unlikely. Let's just do one thing and be alert. Shadow, you should keep an eye on your employees. Especially the ones at high posts. Till then we can try to find out that who will benefit the most with Devil's death." Seena suggested.

"Don't you think we should try and find out who the number belongs to, the one from which the calls were made?", Rohit proposed.

"Devil, I think you know me better than that. I am not one to be careless about such things. I searched for the number, but it belonged to a stranger. I called that person and she said that she had been allotted that number just two days ago. The previous owner had probably canceled his service. And I may have given you the call records, but I cannot find out the name of the previous owner. And I am not sure I want the police's help. Being the famous Malhotra brothers, the news of you taking the help of the police would spread like wildfire. And the culprit would become alert endangering your life even further. Next time, don't you dare think that I am careless because I am not." Seena explained.

"Ok, ok, I am sorry Angel. By the way, why did you call Raj 'Shadow'?" Rohit apologized.

"Mr. Devil, obviously, it's a nickname since Raj is also a part of our group now. And he and Seena are working together to solve this mystery, like partners and so Shadow suits him and the situation." Krutika spoke.

"Oh, ok. Then we can also call him shadow, right?" Rohit asked.

"Yes, you can. And I can also call you Devil! As you are one to me" Raj exclaimed.

"Fine with me and I am not a devil to you." Rohit argued.

"Yeah whatever" Raj said in a dismissive manner.

The four then spent the rest of the evening together, laughing and chatting, and talking about random things.

12
DEVIL'S ENEMIES

It had been a week since all of them had met. There had been no progress in the mystery. Raj was keeping a check on all of his employees, and the four were always alert. Presently, Seena was sitting in her cabin waiting for Krutika and Raj. They had decided to meet and plan their next step. After some time they came.

"Hi" Raj said.

"Hey" "Hi" Seena and Krutika greeted him back.

"Any idea about the mystery?" Krutika asked.

"Not yet" Seena replied.

"Nope" Raj denied. Krutika nodded. They all sat in silence. Everyone was thinking the same thing, who could be the culprit.

"Who could hate Devil so much to go as far as trying to murder him?" Seena spoke.

"We are successful businessmen, we obviously have some rivals, but I am not sure that anyone would go to the extent of murder. And anyway, if it really was a business rival, then I should have been the target, not Rohit. I am the CEO while Rohit is a lawyer. He only ever handles a few company related matters in my absence like when I am working on a case or when I need him to help me out. Overall, I am the main boss of the company. So, it couldn't have been a business rival, but then who was it?" Raj explained his theory.

"I wouldn't jump to conclusions like that. It may still have a rival company, since Devil was also a co-owner. However unlikely it may be, it's not impossible. We need not give all our attention to the idea, but we shouldn't completely ignore it too." Krutika advised.

The others agreed and nodded their heads in yes. Raj was about to say something, but before he could, his phone rang. He checked the caller's ID and found it to be Mr. Sharma's. He immediately answered the call. "Hello?"

"Hello Mr. Raj. I heard about your brother's accident a few days ago. Sorry, I didn't get time to call earlier. I know that you must be under too much pressure already, so why don't you take an extra month to complete the order."

"Are you sure, sir?"

"Yes, I am."

"Thank you, thank you so much."

"It's ok. I hope your brother is feeling better."

"Yes, he is."

"That's great. I had just called to inform you of the extra time and ask about your brother. So, I will end the call now. Bye."

"Bye sir and thank you once again."

"Glad to help." He said and ended the call. Raj was very happy and a bit relieved. He had been stressing out about the order, but now he could relax a bit. He looked at Seena and Krutika and told them the good news. They both were equally happy and congratulated Raj.

"Now that this is settled and you have been given more time, I guess we should focus on the mystery. What should be our next step?" Seena asked.

"I think that we should find out if Rohit has any enemies." Raj suggested.

"I don't think he has. He is always nice to everyone. Even in college, Devil never troubled anyone. And as you said, having a business enemy is unlikely for him. However, there is one aspect that cannot be ignored." Seena said.

"What?" Raj questioned.

"That he is a lawyer, and he may have made some enemies along his way. He has sent many criminals to prison. It is possible that someone wanted to take revenge." Krutika explained.

"You are right. In that case we should check out his files and see if any criminal is out of prison yet." Raj agreed.

"Yes, and I think that this should be done by you, Shadow. You are his brother and a lawyer yourself. You ought to be able to do it." Seena told Raj.

"Ok, I will do it, but what will you both do till then?"

"We will focus on our jobs." Krutika stated. Raj nodded.

"Ok then, I think I will start searching from tomorrow only. And I suggest that we meet after like a week or two, once I am done with my research."

Seema and Krutika agreed. Just as Raj was about to leave, he remembered something.

"Oh, by the way, the police came and questioned Rohit the day before yesterday. They asked some basic questions like if he had enemies or if he doubted someone to do this to him and stuff like that."

"Oh okay. I guess since we already gave them the jeep and the driver, they didn't need to ask about that." Seena assumed,

"Obviously Angel. Anyways thanks for telling us Raj." Krutika thanked him.

"No problem." Raj replied.

Raj bid bye to them and went home. It was already evening, so he just had his dinner and went to sleep. The next day, he went to his brother's study and began searching for his case files. He looked through all of the files and got the information that he needed. Rohit always kept a record of all cases that he took up, in case the criminals tried to harm someone or get in trouble again. Raj learnt that only three out of all the criminals were free right now. He decided to meet them. Not as a lawyer but as a normal, curious and friendly college student who was surveying random people for a project. He changed his clothes and wore some casual ones. He wore a T-shirt and jeans. He noted down the address of the first suspect and left. When he reached it, he rang the bell with a curious look on his face. The door opened a few seconds later and a man dressed in all black, tall and muscular came out. "Yes?", the man said in his hoarse voice.

"Hi, my name is Rohan, I am a college student studying crime journalism. I was hoping you would like to give me an interview since I am doing a survey of random people for a project of mine." Raj said while changing his voice so that he sounded like a fun loving and cheerful student. The man was suspicious at first but got convinced by Raj's story.

"Sure. Ask whatever you want."

"Thank you so much. So, the first question is what is your name and occupation?" Raj asked looking at an empty notepad and pretending to read the questions from there.

"My name is Michael, and I am a gym instructor."

"Ok and what is your opinion on the present law system of our country?"

"I am not in love with it, and it certainly isn't perfect, but I guess it's not the worst either. It is a bit sufficient, I guess."

"Yes, and the last question, please don't take it personally but have you ever had any trouble with the law?"

"Yes, I did. And I got punished for my crimes too."

"Yet you don't seem to hate the law system. How?"

"See, I am not a psycho or something. Once I got jailed, I realized my mistake and became a better person. That's it."

"That's really nice to hear. Well, thank you for your time. I would like to take a leave now. It was nice meeting you. Bye."

"Nice to meet you too. Bye." Michael closed the door as Raj left.

13
INTERVIEWS

Raj then checked his list and went to the next suspect's house. When he reached it, he saw that there was a big mansion with a beautiful garden and three expensive cars standing there. He was really impressed. He went towards the gates and rang the bell. A security guard came rushing towards him and asked him who he was. "I am Rohan, and I am doing a few interviews for my college project. May I please meet Mr. Jaynat the owner of this house, I want to interview him and ask him about his lifestyle."

"Ok, I will ask him if he's available for you." The guard then went inside the house and returned after a few minutes.

"You are lucky he is free right now. Usually, he won't be. Just go straight and there will be a library to your left. You will find him there."

"Thank you." Raj said and went inside. He followed the guard's directions and soon found Jaynat. He was completely engrossed in a book, so Raj cleared his throat so as to make Jaynat aware of his presence. Jaynat stopped reading and looked up at the sound. He saw Raj and gestured to him to take a seat.

"Yes, so how may I help you?"

" Hi sir, my name is Rohan. I am doing a project in which I am interviewing some random people and you happened to be one of them. If you don't mind, then can we start the interview?"

"Sure"

"Thank you, sir. My first question is how is it to have such a rich lifestyle?"

"Well, it is obviously a nice feeling to be able to live with so many luxuries. However, it does sometimes get boring."

" I can understand. Well, being able to live such a luxurious life must have its perks as well as some downfalls. Can you explain any?"

"Yeah. Well one of the perks of being rich is that you can have mostly everything that you could ever need. You almost never need to worry about the expense. You can fulfill all your desires that require money. As for downfalls, I would say that you don't really get good friends or good people around you. Mostly people are just after your money."

"Hmm. I agree, people are very greedy nowadays. However, being so rich also brings some fame. And fame brings fans and haters. And those haters then become the cause of rumors. Please don't mind, but I did hear a rumor about you. Perhaps you would like to clear it so that people won't believe it."

"Ok but isn't your project just a normal college project. Then how is the world going to know if the rumor is true or not?"

"Oh, well if I am able to do all my interviews successfully, I am going to have a chance to publish my project for the world to see."

"Oh okay. Well, what is the rumor, anyway?"

"The rumor is that you are said to have had some trouble with the law. Is that right?", Raj said, in a professional manner.

Jaynat looked surprised. He obviously didn't expect this to be the rumor. He soon came back into his senses and said,

" Well, no that is wrong. It is just a rumor."

"Really? Well, I have reason to believe that it is indeed true. I even happen to have evidence."

"So, if you already know the truth then why did you ask me?"

"I need to. Even if only as a formality. However, I would like to know the reason behind your lie and your encounter with the police."

"Hmm, I guess it won't hurt now that I have left that past behind me. Fine, I will tell you, but it shouldn't come into public. Not this part. Anyway, the thing is that day I was too stressed as I wasn't able to find a job. I had finally gotten a chance in a multinational company, and I was already late for the interview. So, I was driving a bit too fast and accidentally hit someone. However, I was already so tense that I didn't realize it and kept going on. As it would be I not only got selected in that interview but also am the owner of that very company right now. However, when I got home, I found a few police officers waiting for me. They told me about the accident and showed the CCTV from a shop nearby to that place. Since I hadn't even noticed the accident taking place, I had no idea about it and no proof of my innocence. So, they arrested me, and a court case happened. I obviously lost. I had no way of justifying my actions. I knew I was wrong, and eventually I accepted it. Sure, that put my career on the line, but it was my own fault. Once I got out of jail, I had a hard time living in society, but I did not give up. I continued working hard and was finally able to improve my image. After that I wrote to the company again. They had rejected me because of the prison case, but now that I had proven myself, they agreed to hire me. So, I got hired and eventually climbed my way up until I became the CEO. That's it."

"Well, I think your story is a very inspiring one. Thank you so much for your time. I'll take your leave now." Raj said and left. The next and the last suspect was a girl. She lived in a dorm room as a paying guest. When he reached there, he saw a few bells. He rang one and waited at the door. Soon a man in his seventies with a walking stick came out. The man looked at Raj up and down.

"Umm, hi, my name is Rohan, and I am here to meet Shrina. Do you know which floor...".

Before Raj could complete his question, the man started hitting Raj with his walking stick. "No men allowed in girls room. No men allowed in girls room. No men allowed in girls room." The man kept repeating.

"Ahh, ouch, aah. Sorry, ow, s.sorry uncle." Raj was in pain. He somehow managed to run away and immediately left the place in his car. After reaching a bit far, he stopped, and called Seena and told her about everything that had happened since they had last met. "So, I checked two of the suspects and they seem fine. However, I couldn't check the last one as it was a girl, and she lives in a paying guest room. The bell I rang must have belonged to the landlord and he won't allow me to meet her. He even hit me with his stick. Only I know how I escaped. Please help me and come and interview the suspect. You are a girl so surely, he will let you in.", he explained to her.

"Ok, ok. I will do it. Why don't you come pick me up?"

"Ok, I am coming. Bye and thanks."

"I have to do it, for Rohit, for Krits, for me and for you. Bye." She cut the call, but Raj was lost in his own thoughts. The moment she had said 'for you' his mind had stopped working. He came back to his senses when his phone vibrated. He looked at it and realized that Seena had already hung up and that the vibration was from a random notification. He kept his phone back in his pocket and started driving towards the hospital.

14

LIGHT

The two went back to the dorm. Seena got out and rang a bell. As it would be, the person who opened the door was the suspect. "Hi, myself Sheila. I am a law student and am doing some random interviews. I actually found your name while looking at some random case files. I hope that you will be able to spend some time and give me an interview."

Shrina looked at Seena from head to toe as if not convinced by her story. "If I spend my valuable time on you, what do I get in return?" Seena was taken aback. She had not expected this response. However, she quickly composed herself and replied,

" I could pay you."

"How much are we talking?"

"Five hundred?"

"Are you kidding me? No."

"One thousand?"

"Nope"

"Two thousand? That's all I can give you. If you want, you can earn some extra money or waste your time doing and earning nothing."

Shrina thought for a moment and slowly began nodding her head. "Ok but ask the questions outside only. I am not letting you inside my house."

"Sure." They both moved a bit to the outside. "So, I will not waste any time with any silly questions and will get straight to the point. As I said earlier, I found your name in a case file. Could you please expand on exactly what were the accusations made against you and how you feel about them and the final verdict of the case?"

Shrina frowned but answered. "I was accused of stealing my ex-boyfriend's car after he supposedly left me with the reason that I am a gold digger. I think that the accusations made no sense. I mean sure he had said that he wanted to break up with me, but he just left in between our conversation. I mean I had just paused to take a sip of my coffee and he left, saying that I didn't want to pay attention to him even when he was breaking up and he was fed up. So, nothing was confirmed as our conversation was left incomplete. True we didn't talk for months after that, but that didn't mean that we broke up. He was still my boyfriend, and I had all rights over his car. So, what wrong did I do? As for the verdict, it was unfair too. When I tried to explain, they said that I made no sense and that he had clearly given me a reason and broken up with me. I mean when, how? Anyway, so yeah, the whole case was unfair and because of that I now have to live here in the small apartment. "

" So, you are holding grudges against your ex and the court and judge and lawyer. Since you think that everyone was unfair."

"Of course I am holding a grudge, but it's mostly against my ex. Sure, I am really angry with the judge and the lawyer too because they didn't believe me, and I sure hope that they regret it, but I don't really care about them. So yeah."

"Hmm. Ok. That's it. Thank you for your not so precious time."

"What the hell? I helped you and you have no manners to express your gratitude. I did you a favor. You owe me one."

"Girl, in your dreams. I owe you nothing. And if you can hear, then I did just thank you."

"You know you are going to get an A in your project because of me, right? And this is how you treat me? So disrespectful."

"I haven't even started disrespecting you. As for the project, I am not going to include your interview because I don't want to fail for having your dumb responses in my file."

"Dumb? How dare you? For your kind information, I am way smarter than you."

"Your IQ is so low you didn't even make it to the bell curve's lowest category. Infact talking to you is dropping my IQ level."

"You know what? It's not your fault. Clearly you were born this stupid."

"And clearly you were born without common sense. Anyways, I don't feel like wasting my time on you anymore. So, I am going to go but before I do, let me tell you one thing. Your ex is a great man and he deserves a Nobel prize for dealing with your nonsense. I truly wish him the best in life an for you, the opposite. Bye crazy lady."

Seena said and immediately left while Shrina was speechless. She angrily stomped her foot and went back inside the building. Seena went to the car and got in.

She told everything to Raj. When she finished, Raj was laughing. "You are always so savage, but I love it." He smiled. Seena blushed a bit but immediately hid it.

"Want me to shower you with my savageness too? ", she asked.

"No, no, I am sorry. Well, she is not the one either. So, what's next? "

"For now, just keep an eye out for anything suspicious in your company. Other than that, try to think of other reasons why someone might want to attack Devil."

"Ok. Should I drop you at your home or hospital?"

"Hospital. I have another surgery left for today."

"Okay."

They both drove to the hospital. "Hey, do you want me to pick you up once you're done?" Raj asked as Seena was getting out.

"Why do you suddenly want to become my personal driver?"

Raj rolled his eyes. "Oh, come on, I was just trying to be a good friend and help you. Since your car is with the police for inspection."

"Well, my good friend, I have Kruts to drop me. We live close to each other. So, thanks for your offer but I won't accept it."

"Ok Light."

"Light?"

"Yup, your new nickname. Since Rohit and Krits already call you Angel, I thought it wouldn't be fair if I suddenly started calling you that too. So, I came up with a nickname of my own."

"Ok, but why Light?"

"It's actually really simple. We are partners and my nickname is Shadow. However, a shadow is not possible without a source of light. So that's why."

Seena was really touched and felt some unknown feeling in her heart, but she didn't understand them. While on the other hand Raj was thinking about what he just said. He was shocked at himself. He was unable to understand how he came up with a new nickname for Seena, so suddenly and with a reasoning like that. They both were silent as neither knew what to say next. Finally, Seena broke the silence.

"Umm..t-thanks. I-I have to go now. I need to prepare for the surgery. See you soon. Bye." She immediately ran off. Raj found this cute and chuckled. He also drove off towards his home. For the next few days, Raj kept a close eye on all of his employees, but he found nothing suspicious. He was getting frustrated. He couldn't think why anyone would try to harm his brother. He decided to talk with Seena and see if she had any ideas. He called her.

"Hi Light."

"Hi Shadow. Why did you call? What happened?"

"Wow. I don't know whether to be impressed or upset. You straightaway got to the point without even asking how am I."

"Sorry, how are you?"

"I am fine, what about you?"

"Me too. Now tell me why you called?"

"Well, I have been keeping a close eye on my company and my staff, but I didn't find anything strange or suspicious and I am getting frustrated because it's been so long, and I don't have a single clue as to who's the culprit. Please tell me that you have an idea."

"Unfortunately, no I don't. However, I can suggest one thing. It's been quite some time since you have been watching your employees and if you haven't found anything yet, then I think it's safe to at least assume for now that it is no one from your company and it was probably a setup. So, the next step should be to see who has a motive."

"I know, you said that last time too, but I couldn't think of anyone."

"It's ok. I will help. Let's see, the law angle was a fail. So now we get into the business angle."

"How? If it were to be the business angle, the target should have been me, not him. I am the CEO, not him." Raj almost shouted.

"Calm down, calm down. Take a deep breath." Raj did as she said. "Good, now listen to me. Yes, you are the CEO, but Devil is also the President. Plus, his accident did cause you some trouble, didn't it? So, I think that it is very much possible. Just try and look into it."

"Now that I think about it, you are right. And infact I do know someone who will go to any extent to harm my company."

15
A REAL SUSPECT

"Then what are you waiting for? Go and check on that person. Now."

"Okay as you say. I will cut the call then. Bye Light."

"Bye Shadow."

They both cut the call. Raj quickly opened his laptop and began his research. For the next two days, Raj was almost always on his laptop. He was still digging into any information he could find related to that person and was trying to confirm his doubts. Finally, he was done. However, he was confused about something. He decided to call Seena and Kritika at his home to discuss his findings. The girls agreed and they all met up at Raj and Rohit's house in the evening.

"What happened Shadow?" Seena asked.

"Yeah, what happened Raj?" Rohit also had no idea.

"Okay, so I did some research about that guy I was talking about, Light. And now I have found another guy's name that I feel I have heard somewhere but where, I don't remember." Raj began.

Seena was about to say something bit Rohit spoke first. "Two things. No. 1 Who is Light? No.2 What guys? What are you talking about?"

"I will explain. So basically, Light is the nickname given to me by Shadow. And about two days ago he had called me, and we discussed the whole case, when he remembered about someone who could go to any extent to harm you guys. Now Shadow, what is this guy's name, and who is this other guy?" Seena explained.

Rohit nodded, understanding everything. Whereas Raj answered Seena. "The guy is actually the owner of our biggest rival company, The Singhania Industries. His name is Garan, and the other guy is his son, Pankit, who is the new CEO of the company after his father."

"Oh okay. Wait, you said Pankit, right? Is it possible that it is the same Pankit whom I had rejected in college? He even had the same surname." Seena questioned.

"You are right. So that is where I heard Pankit. Thanks."

"Hmm. Wait, Kru, what was the name of the boy who Rohit had beaten out of jealousy?" Seena inquired from her friend.

"Umm, I think his name was Pankit too and his dad was a businessman." Krutika replied.

"Meaning, he was the same person as there was only one Pankit in our college that year. In that case, if he was your friend, why would he harm your boyfriend? Hadn't he already forgiven Rohit too?" Seena asked no one in particular.

"May I say something?" Rohit said suddenly.

"Sure", the other three spoke in unison.

"Okay, so even if he didn't forgive me then or even if he didn't care that I was his friend's boyfriend. Why would he try to kill me for such a small reason?"

"The reason may be bigger than you think Rohit. Do not forget that he is also the CEO of our rival company. Maybe that combined with the rest is the reason." Raj suggested.

"Then why not you? Why me? You are the CEO. Not me. Yes, I am the so-called President, but my accident didn't cause many problems, right? I mean you are still able to run the company. Even if Angel and Queenie had not been there to help you, you would still have been able to run the business. Yes, you would have been under immense pressure, but you would have been able to do it. I was just overseeing the work in the factory. Anyone could do that. Plus, the factory could still be run without a supervisor. The workers are trustworthy. The supervisor's only job is to take orders, handle any problem that arises, and be a formal leader, that's it. So why?" Rohit was still perplexed.

"No idea", Raj admitted.

"I know it does not make complete sense, but it still seems a bit logical. I think there is something else that we are missing, something that we don't know about. And we must find that out quick. As of now, he is our only real suspect and Shadow, please keep an eye out for that him, okay?" Seena advised. The others agreed and Seena and Krutika left. Raj turned to his brother and said,

"By the way, I believe I forgot to say this, but your choice is actually really good. Krutika is a lovely girl. Well done bro."

"Thanks, but I think that your girlfriend is also pretty good. Good work bro."

"My girlfriend? Who?"

"Angel obviously. Who else?"

"And why would you think that she is my girlfriend?"

"You are not too fond of pet names. You literally never even gave me a nickname. Though you didn't hesitate to give her one. That too such a cute one, Light. Just like she gave you one and you never objected. Also, Shadow cannot exist without Light. Isn't it obvious that you two are a couple?"

"No, it isn't, because we aren't a couple. Now go and take a rest."

"Oh, okay, if you say so. Maybe I just predicted the future in that case."

"I said GO."

"Okay, okay, I am going. Chill out. Bye."

He left from there while Raj started thinking about his words and sat on the couch. 'Maybe I just predicted the future' 'you didn't hesitate to give her one.' 'not too fond of pet names' 'Just like she gave you one and you never objected' 'Isn't it obvious that you two are a couple?' Raj couldn't get rid of his thoughts. The only thing roaming in his mind was whether Rohit was right and was he really going to be together with Seena in the future? He didn't know, but somewhere in his heart he wanted it to be true.

16
A NEW PROBLEM

For the next few days, no one thought about the mystery. All of them were busy in their own lives. One day, Raj was on his computer when he decided to check the Singhania Company's website. He opened it and was shocked. He saw many of his own designs on the website. Not only that, but he also noticed that they suddenly had many customers. They had amazing reviews and ratings. More than half of their products were on the verge of being sold out. He went on the internet and searched for more information. He found that the company had risen from the ashes. A year ago, it was barely able to maintain enough business to remain as the second-best textile company, it was now making tons of profit. It was also speculated that they may become no. 1 soon if their rate of success does not decrease. Raj was confused. Recently, their situation had worsened. It had started getting bad reviews and was barely making any profits. It lost its position and was now 12th out of 15, in the industry. Some people even believed that it would go bankrupt soon and now suddenly it was making profits in lakhs and its reputation, which had been damaged, was now completely restored. However, one thing scared him. There was a rumor that the contract he had gotten may be given to them instead. He immediately conference called Seena, Rohit and Krutika and told them everything. Their reactions were not much different from his.

"The heck. How did this happen overnight?" Seena asked.

"Exactly, it's not possible." Krutika added.

"I know but it has already happened apparently. Though I can't understand how?" Rohit said.

"Guess their new CEO is good for them." Raj reasoned.

"Maybe, but wasn't he the Pankit from our college? You know what we had just guessed at that time. Raj do one thing and sent us a picture of this boy. Let's first confirm if he is actually the same person." Rohit suggested.

Raj agreed and sent the picture to everyone. When Seena and Krutika saw the picture, they confirmed that it was indeed the same person. However, Rohit was quiet, which was surprising since this while picture thing was his idea.

"Rohit, what happened? Why are you so quiet?" Raj inquired.

"I just noticed something." Rohit replied.

"What?" All three said in unison.

"The tattoo on his hand, left hand to be precise. On the back of his palm, a black dragon symbol. I have seen that before." Rohit answered.

"Where have you seen it?" Krutika questioned.

"On the man's hand who had tried to touch you wrongly, Queenie."

"Are you sure?" Seena wanted to confirm as she was shocked.

"Yes, I am 100% sure. Though it was dark, and I couldn't see his face, when I was hitting him, he tried to protect himself and I saw that tattoo. His hands were covering his face, so I couldn't see it." Rohit said with affirmation.

Krutika was speechless. Finally, after processing and realizing everything, she spoke,

"So, the man who proposed to Angel, the one whom you punched out of jealousy, my friend, the one who tried to touch me inappropriately and you beat him up and the CEO of your biggest rival company are all the same person?"

"Yes darling." Rohit replied.

"Well, this clears up the mystery. It was obviously he who did all this. We just need proof now." Seena acclaimed.

"How is it obviously him? I mean I know that him being in your life since college and being literally everywhere is suspicious, but it doesn't confirm that he is the criminal that we are looking for." Raj didn't understand Seena's point.

"I will tell you. I have a theory. See, during college days, you were in London, so Rohit was the one helping your dad in company matters. And Pankit was helping his dad. Since he saw Devil helping your dad, he may have assumed that he is the next CEO. Also, he wanted Krutika but couldn't get her and instead got beaten up by Devil and lost Kru, to him. So obviously he was angry. When he tried to befriend her, Devil punched him which would have only made him angrier. As for me, when I rejected him, he must have been furious, and when he saw that Kruts and I were with Devil, talking and laughing, his temper must have worsened. And to add fuel to the fire,

Devil was doing really good in life and is the son of his dad's biggest rival company's owner. So even if he knew that, you, Raj, are the CEO now, he had a lot of other things against Rohit who is still the president of your company. Not to forget, your company was the reason his dad's business was suffering. If put this way, it all makes sense." Seena explained. Everyone thought for some time and then Raj spoke,

"I think you have something there, Light. You may be right."

"I agree. You are probably right, and the theory makes sense." Kru agreed.

"I am also with you. Even I think that you are right but as you said we need proof." Rohit said.

"Yes, and we are going to gather it. Shadow and Devil, talk to your dad, get as much information about your rival company as possible and Shadow, I think that there is something suspicious in the way they rose to success overnight. Find out the truth. Meanwhile, me and Kru will search our college website and find out Pankit's history and take care of your order." Seena ordered.

Everyone was fine with their tasks, so they cut the call. As soon as the call ended, Raj got a call from Mr. Sharma. He immediately answered.

"Hello"

"Hello Raj. How are you and your brother?"

"We both are absolutely fine sir and Rohit is recovering pretty well."

"That's good to know. Coming to the point, Raj, you must have seen the latest news about the Singhanias."

"Yes, I have sir and it's very surprising."

"Surprising indeed but a good outcome for them. I think that their new CEO has talent and capability. So,

I have decided to distribute the order. Half of it you are going to complete, and the other half will be completed by Singhania Industries. It will also reduce your stress and workload."

"Sir, I can complete the order on my own. I have people who are helping me. Rohit's accident has caused some personal pain and problems, but the company and business haven't suffered much. I assure you that I can handle it. Trust me you do not need to distribute the order."

" It's not that I doubt you, Raj. I don't. It's good that you have people helping you, but they can only do so much. You are the main person, and you have many responsibilities. Plus, as you yourself just said, the accident caused you some personal pain, and I understand. Such things tend to impact one's mental health. I just want to reduce the work pressure on you so that you can relax and take care of your brother. I am just giving you a chance to come back stronger. This incident has to have some of your attention which means that you cannot fully focus on your business right now, which I am not complaining about. I am just saying that I only want to help. Also, if their company can achieve such fame and success in such a little time, they would surely do justice to my order. You don't need to worry and just complete half the order. And this would also help complete the order in less than two months. See you soon. Bye."

"Yes sir. Bye." Raj ended the call. He sighed and sat down on his chair. Not only had Pankit done so much to his friends and family but now he was harming the business too. This had to be stopped. The truth had to come out.

17

CONFIRMED

Raj immediately went back to his computer and began digging deeper. He searched every source of information about the Singhania enterprises that he could find. Every article about their failure and their sudden rise to fame. Something was bugging him but exactly what he just couldn't point out. He kept thinking but nothing came to him though he had a feeling that all his answers were right in front of him. He also needed to speed up the process of the production of the order and complete it, not half but full. He texted Seena and Krutika to come to his factory as soon as possible and left for the factory himself. After arriving, he went inside and ordered all the workers to leave work for a minute and gather in front of the cabin as he had an announcement to make.

"Everyone, as you all know, Rohit has had an accident and won't be back for quite some time. Some of my friends have been helping out. However, you all are the real workers. You make the production process possible. You work so hard to make one piece of cloth and your hard work is much appreciated. So now, I have a request to make. Due to some problems, we have to complete our latest order sooner than expected. I hope at least some of you are willing to work overtime, paid of course. Please, I really need your help and I promise a huge bonus if you are able to accomplish this. The new time limit is that you have to complete the whole order in one and a half months. Please."

The workers looked at each other and one of them spoke, " Sir, we understand your situation and although we can't promise it, but we will try our best to complete the order as soon as we can."

"Thank you so much. I am really grateful. Now you all may go back to your work. If you face any problems, please contact me immediately." The workers agreed and went away. Just then Seena and Krutika came there.

"Shadow, what happened? Why did you call us so urgently?" Seena asked.

"Yes Raj, why?" Krutika added.

" Girls, I am in a big fix right now. Mr. Sharma, the one who gave me the order, has now given half of the order to the Singhania enterprises. Looks like we were right. Rohit's accident did do them a lot of good." Raj explained.

"I knew it. It's all because of that bloody Pankit. Shadow what is our plan?" Seena was getting angry at Pankit.

"Firstly, I want to complete the whole order as soon as possible so that once we expose him, Mr. Sharma doesn't face any problems. Even though he did take away half the order from me, his intentions weren't bad. And I respect him a lot." Raj stated.

"Okay, you don't need to worry about that. I will handle it. Also, is this Mr. Sharma by any chance the manager of KS Companies?" Krutika questioned.

"Yes, he is. Do you know him?" Raj confirmed.

"Nope, just asking." Krutika shrugged.

"Okay, but how are you going to manage everything alone? We will help." Raj offered.

"No, no need. Trust me, I can do this. Just give me one second. I need to make a phone call." Krutika said and left. She called someone and talked to him for about ten minutes and then came back.

"Well, are you really sure? You are a dentist. Not that I am saying that you are not capable. You are, but you also need to handle your patients. Who is going to do that?" Seena was not so sure about the plan.

"Don't worry my dear Angel. I am absolutely sure and as for my patients, I may be a bit favored as a dentist, but the others are well capable too. I am sure they can take care of it whenever I am unavailable. Also, I insist." Krutika answered.

"Okay then. I don't mind. Anyways, Light and Kruts, there is one more thing. I researched a lot about Pankit's company, and everything seemed perfect. It seemed all good. I could feel that there was something that was right in front of my eyes, but I couldn't identify it." Raj told the whole story and about all that he found out.

"I agree, it is all good, too good to be true infact." Seena agreed.

Raj's eyes widened. "You are right. Thank you, thank you, thank you so much Light. I finally know what it was that was troubling me."

"What?" Seena was confused.

"It is all too good to be true. It cannot be real. That is our clue. Now we need to find evidence." Raj was happy now. Seeing him so happy, a smile crept on Seena's face. Raj, in his excitement hugged Seena and kissed her cheeks, completely forgetting everything else. However, he soon realized and backed away while looking down.

Seena was taken aback by his actions and was blushing very hard. She tried but failed to hide her red face. She also looked away. Krutika, who sensed what was going on, became extremely happy and excited for her friends. However, to remove the awkwardness, she faked a cough.

"Umm, I think we should go now. Kruts, if you want you can stay and have a look at the factory and the whole production process. I think we should maintain secrecy. We cannot let anyone know that we are going to do the whole order. Pankit needs to believe that he is winning so that he lets his guard down and gives us a chance to trap him. So please, both of you be mindful of that. Anyways, here are the keys to the factory, Kruts. You need to lock the door after everyone leaves or you can leave before also as the door is password protected and locks by itself. The keys are just an extra precaution. In case we ever forget the password. Or if the system fails. Also, the password is engraved on the keys. See you later. Bye."

Raj explained everything and then left with Seena. Once outside, Seena said, "Shadow, don't you think that Kruts is acting a bit suspicious. I mean I understand that she wants to help but even to me she never mentioned knowing anything about business. I knew she had a relative who is a businessman, and yes, she attended a few classes in college with me, but as far as I remember, she never paid attention in those classes. So, her confidence is surprising as she has no experience either. "

"Even I thought that it's strange but she was insisting on it so much and she really wanted to do it so I agreed. I think we should just trust her and wait."

"I guess you are right. Anyway, now that one problem is taken care of, what do you want to do next?"

"I have an idea, but I am not sure if it will work or if I should even do it."

"What is the idea?"

"You have to go and meet Pankit. He did propose to you once and maybe he won't mind if you come into his life again. You need to go and talk to him and get the truth out, while I record it. However, I am not sure if it is a good idea. He can be dangerous, and I don't want you to get hurt because of me."

Seena was quiet for a moment. "I will do it. It is a great plan. And you don't need to worry about me. I know self-defense. Plus, you will be there too. Right? So, you can save me if need be. The only question is how can I meet him?"

"If you say so, then alright. Let's do it. Just wait a bit and I will work out all the details and tell you. It will take about a week most probably."

"Ok."

They both smiled at each other and went their own ways after bidding bye to each other. During the whole week, Raj kept a close eye on Pankit's activities through the help of the media. He knew that this sudden rise to fame is going to get a lot of attention and so is the new CEO. As he had suspected, many journalists caught Pankit at a restaurant on Saturday. In reply to one of the questions asked, Pankit stated that he went to that restaurant every Saturday, without fail. This was the information Raj was waiting for. Now all he had to do was tell Seena about this and she would handle the rest. He called Seena.

"Hey Light. I have some good news. Pankit goes to a restaurant called Simple Serve restaurant every Saturday without fail. So, all you have to do is go there this upcoming Saturday. I will also be there."

"That's great. You should book a table for two immediately."

"Ok and thanks once again for helping. I love you."

"What?"

Raj's eyes widened as he realized what he had said. "I... I mean as a friend, a partner."

"Yeah of course." Seena felt disappointed for some reason unknown to her. They quickly cut the call to prevent any further awkwardness.

18
PROOF

As soon as she ended the call, Seena started thinking about what just happened. She was confused as to why she felt upset and sad when Raj said that he only loved her as a friend. They were only friends, then why did it hurt? She didn't love him, or did she? She wasn't completely sure. On the other side, Raj was also thinking about what he said and why he said it. He knew that he didn't mean it when he said that he only loved her as a friend, but what more could it be? Somewhere in his heart, he knew the answer, it was love. However, he was not ready to accept that he fell in love with his friend. A few days passed, and during these days Raj helped Seena prepare for her encounter with Pankit. It was Friday. Raj and Seena were at his office in his company. "Light, are you ready for tomorrow?"

"I am. You don't need to worry. I can handle this."

"I know you can. I believe in you but just don't try to shower him with your savageness."

"Okay, okay, I won't. I would shower him with love instead. Is that fine?"

"No need to do that, just flirt a bit and make him spill out the truth."

"Yeah, but I can only do that if I show him that I love him."

"I said no." Raj shouted.

Seena was shocked. "Why? Are you perhaps jealous?"

Now it was Raj who looked shocked. "No, I am not. Why would I be? I just said that as he is clearly not a good guy, and you are my friend. That is all.", he said and looked away.

"Okay, if you say so.", she was not convinced.

The next day Seena went to the restaurant as planned and saw Raj, disguised, sitting on the table next to Pankit. She went towards Pankit and pretended to be surprised to see him there.

"Hi Pankit, remember me?" Pankit looked up from his phone and saw Seena.

"Seena? The girl who rejected me in front of the whole campus?"

"Oh, come on, forget it now. You were full of attitude back then, but when you became Krutika's friend, I kind of regretted rejecting you and that's why I behaved nicely with you."

"Oh really, I thought you did all that for Krutika's sake."

"Well, I didn't, I did it for myself."

"That's good to know. Have a seat." Seena sat.

"How come you never told me you liked me?" Pankit asked.

"Oh, I never had the guts to after doing what I did. I thought you would hate me."

"I didn't and could never hate such a beautiful girl like you." Pankit kept his hand on Seena's. Seeing this, Raj was getting jealous.

"Oh, I am so good to know that."

"By the way, how are you here?"

"Oh, I just wanted to try a new place and came here for a meal."

"Ok. Do you want to order something?"

"Yeah, a cheeseburger would be fine."

"As you wish my lady." He called the waiter and ordered. The waiter went away. "So, what do you do?"

"I am a doctor and if I am not wrong you are the best businessman in town." She winked at him.

"Are you trying to flirt with me?"

"Can't I? I thought you loved me."

"I still do, just that I was surprised to the savage queen of our college flirting with me."

"I am savage for everyone else but not for the person closest to my heart."

"I am not sure I am that person though."

"Believe me you are."

"Make me believe it "

"As you wish, my king"

She leaned to his side, and gently touched his cheeks. She looked in his eyes and leaned a bit closer. She whispered in his ears, "Do you trust me now, my hot hero."

She backed up a bit and touched his lips with her thumb while smiling seductively. Then she sat back down in her seat. Raj was astonished. He was burning in anger. 'This is too much. How can she do that knowing that I am right here?' he kept thinking. While Pankit and Seena, Pankit was quite surprised too.

"I guess I have to believe you now. Don't I sweetie?"

Seena nodded.

"You know recently I heard that your company rose to fame overnight, under your guidance. I must say, I am very impressed."

"Oh well, thank you. What about Rohit though, how is he? I heard he had an accident."

"I lost contact with him after college, so I don't know how he is, and I don't even care."

"That's strange. Didn't you used to like him? You were always smiling and laughing whenever you were with him."

"He was just a friend, baby. And when he punched you, I hated him after that. However, I couldn't show it because I was worried that he would harm you further. So, I kept an eye on him for you."

"Really? Thank you so much Seenu."

"Anything for you."

Seena was feeling extremely annoyed, but she had to do this. "I am shocked to know all this but very grateful at the same time. If you still love me, would you like to go on a date after this?" Seena was about to answer when her burger arrived.

Once the waiter left, she continued. "Of course. And in any case who wouldn't want to date a guy like you? You have everything, a kind heart, a sweet personality, a handsome face and even money. I am sure you must have worked so hard to save your business and I am so glad you did it. You know what, why don't you tell me how you achieved such a big feat. I am sure I will love the story."

"Fine but are you sure you are not in touch with anybody, not even Krutika?"

"I am not, believe me. You can check my phone if you want."

"I think I will." Seena gave him her phone.

Pankit checked her contacts and there was no contact of Rohit or Krutika. He checked her messages too but found nothing. He also checked her Instagram and gallery but failed to find anything suspicious. There were no pics of any guys either. It was only her dad and himself.

"I can see that you are telling the truth. Okay then, I will tell you how I did it."

"Yes, please."

"Okay, so now I will impress you more, darling, by telling you, my secret."

"Please do, I really want to know how you defeated those Malhotra Industries."

"I didn't really do much. I worked hard, trusted my workers, and that's it. I was just really lucky I guess."

"Lucky? How?"

"Lucky because I noticed Raj listening to us and recording our conversation. And also, because I saw him fuming in jealousy while looking at us. Your game is over. I know everything. I know all your plans to collect evidence against me. I know why you came here today. It wasn't by chance, it was all perfectly planned, but you forgot that I have connections too. And I have been keeping an eye on you. Too bad, you came to trap me but got trapped yourself instead."

"Huh? W... What?"

Raj was shocked. This was a dreadful turn of events. Before he could even process what was happening, someone covered his face with a handkerchief drenched in chloroform. He fainted instantly. Pankit did the same with Seena and she lost consciousness too.

19
RECORDING

Pankit had reserved the whole restaurant as he knew that this would happen. Therefore, nobody witnessed him kidnap Raj and Seena. He took them to a basement, tied their hands and feet and locked them inside. When they woke up, they could barely see anything as there was only a single lamp in the middle of the huge basement. Raj woke up first.

"Ugh, this headache is killing me. Where am I?" he groaned. As soon he realized what had happened, he thought of Seena. "Seena? Seena, are you there? Seena? Light?"

"Ugh, Sh...Shadow" Seena woke up.

"Light, are you okay?"

"Yeah, I am fine, what about you?"

"I am alright. Where are you? I cannot see you. It's too dark in here."

"Come near the lamp. Try to drag yourself. I am moving towards it too."

"Okay."

The two managed to drag themselves towards the lamp. They could finally see each other.

"What do we do now?", Seena asked.

"We could…"

Before he could continue, the door opened, and Pankit entered.

"Looks like the little rats woke up. Say hello to your new home guys. Where you are going to live for the rest of your life, which by the way won't be too long since I will starve you both to death."

Raj and Seena looked at each other. Seena turned towards Pankit and spoke, "Pankit, why are you doing this?"

"Oh, you know very well why I am doing this. It's because of you and your Devil and his girlfriend, of course. And Raj is my business rival. My company almost went bankrupt because of him. I had to do something and that was to destroy all of you. "

"You think you are quite clever huh? Well, you are not. I promise that whatever game you are trying to play over here, you won't win. I will make sure of that." Raj declared.

"Do you really think that you are in the position to threaten me? You are way dumber than I expected. Anyways, Seena, sweetie, you asked me how I revived my company so well, right? Well, you know what, I will tell you. Since you are going to die anyways, it cannot cause any harm.

It's all a lie. I haven't revived anything, it's just plain and simple window dressing. My company is in a lot of debt that I can't afford to pay. So, I created a lie, that it is actually doing very well. All these investors, these extra profits, success, good ratings and amazing reviews are all a façade meant to give the creditors a sense of security so that they do not disturb me. All I need is the order from KS Companies, which I have finally received. Though it's only half for now, I am going to convince them to entrust me with it completely. Once I get and complete that order, I will be No. 1 in the industry. I will actually be able to save my company. I will be rich and famous. And I won't have to worry about peasants like you. Now tell me, aren't I smart?"

"No, you are not. Infact you are really stupid. Now don't ask me why. I won't tell you now, but I will show you soon." Raj replied.

"How? From heaven? Keep dreaming. I will go now. And don't forget, that I am the one who caused Rohit's accident. If I can paralyze him, I can kill you too. Have a painful last few days. I wish I could end you know but I don't want blood on my hands. It is what it is, I guess. Goodbye." Pankit left.

Raj and Seena didn't say a word for the next few minutes. Once they were sure that they were alone in the building and that no one could hear them, they began laughing.

"I can't believe he fell for that." Raj whispered in between laughs.

"I know. He really is a brainless fool. Did he really think he did all this? Oh my god I can't stop laughing." Seena answered back, also in whispers, just to be safe.

"Same here."

Raj took a deep breath and stopped laughing. He took off his left shoe. Seena saw this and turned serious. She took out her hairpin and gave it to Raj. He opened the heel of his shoe and pressed a button that was fixed inside. It was a bit above the base of the heel so that it couldn't be activated accidentally while walking. Once he was done, Raj put the heel back in place and wore his shoe again. He gave the pin back to Seena.

"Done. Now he is doomed." Raj smirked.

"He sure is but let's get out of here now." Seena suggested.

"Yeah"

The two got up and went towards the door. Raj put his ears on the door and tried to listen. He could hear some footsteps. He looked through the keyhole and saw a man who looked like a sumo wrestler standing guard. He turned to Seena.

"Oh no. There is a sumo wrestler outside. How will we escape? We did not think this through."

"Yes, we did. Now watch this."

Seena used her hairpin to pick the lock and the door opened with a click. The wrestler heard this and opened the door but was surprised when he saw no one inside. Seena and Raj had hidden behind the door. The minute he stepped foot in the room to check, Seena attacked a nerve on his neck, rendering him unconscious. The sumo fell on the ground but upon Seena's right foot.

"Ahh, my foot." Seena screamed in pain.

Raj bent down and tried to remove her foot from under him but failed. He then used all his strength to roll the sumo and succeeded.

"Ouch, my foot. It hurts so bad Shadow." Seena cried.

'I know, I know my Light. Don't worry, your Shadow is here. I will take care of everything."

He picked her up in bridal style and ran out of the basement.

On the other hand, Rohit and Krutika were at home, in Rohit's study room watching and recording everything through the help of the camera on Seena's shirt button. When Seena's foot got stuck, they got tensed.

"Devil, look. Angel's foot is stuck." Krutika was worried about her friends.

"Don't worry Queenie. See, Raj is there to help her." Rohit assured her.

When Raj finally managed to get Seena free and carried her, they were relieved.

"You were right, Devil. She is fine because Light has her Shadow to protect her." Krutika smiled.

"And Angel is there to save her Shadow. They wouldn't have escaped had it not been for her quick thinking." Rohit responded.

"True. They are made for each other, but they don't know it yet."

"Exactly. Anyways, I will save this recording in my pen drive. Then we can give it to the police."

"Yes, but we should go see Seena first. I am sure Raj must have taken her to Safe n Care hospital only. Let's go."

"Okay."

Rohit saved the recording and pocketed the pen drive. They left for the hospital. Krutika was right. Raj and Seena were there only. They were just coming out of the hospital when Rohit and Krutika reached.

"Raj, Seena, over here." Rohit shouted as soon as he saw them.

"Rohit, Krutika. We are coming." Raj shouted back.

Seena was limping because of the pain and Raj was helping her. Her foot was bandaged but it still hurt to walk.

"What happened?" Krutika asked once they came to them.

"Nothing serious. It's just a sprain. It will heal soon. Till then I can keep limping I guess because I don't want to use crutches or something." Seena explained.

"Are you serious? Seena, you should know better than anyone to not put pressure on an injury. You always keep complaining to me that your patients don't listen to you, but you are not listening to the doctor either. You will use crutches and it's final." Krutika was annoyed.

"I don't need them." Seena defended herself.

"Calm down the both of you. We are outside a hospital, don't start arguing here. Kruts, you don't need to worry. I will take care of Seena. If she doesn't want to use crutches, it's fine. I will carry her to wherever she wants." Raj tried to deescalate the situation as he feared it might get worse.

Seena looked at him, astounded. Raj gave her a look that said, 'Don't worry, I am here. I will take care of you.'

Seena was touched and smiled. Rohit and Krutika secretly awed at the sight of the two.

"Let's go now. I don't think Pankit's men will follow us right now. So, it's better that we go back to the house an discuss our next step." Rohit suggested.

The others agreed and they all went back. At the house, Raj carried Seena, while Krutika pushed Rohit's wheelchair. They sat in Raj's room. Raj placed Seena on the bed an sat with her, placing her foot on his lap so as to give it an elevated height to reduce the swelling, as suggested by the doctor. Krutika also sat down after placing Rohit beside her seat.

"Now there are two things that can be done. No. 1, we give the recording to the police or No. 2, we wait and show it to Mr. Sharma first. What do we do?" Seena inquired.

"I think we should give it to the police as soon as possible. They can handle the rest on their own and can provide us protection too, once Pankit finds out we are missing." Raj advised.

"You are right. That is our best option. And I think we should act upon it immediately." Rohit concurred.

"Okay then. What are we waiting for? Let's go." Krutika stood up from her seat.

"I think you and I should go Kruts. Seena and Rohit should stay back. Rohit has still not recovered completely, and Seena is hurt too." Raj recommended.

"Fine with me." Krutika accepted the idea.

Rohit and Seena were reluctant at first, but then conceded. Raj and Krutika left.

Just as they had stepped out of the house, Raj received a call from Pankit. He was confused and worried that their plan had failed. He answered the call.

"Hello Raj." Pankit greeted.

"What do you want?" Raj questioned.

"You know, you had almost succeeded but I outsmarted you. All of you. I was doubtful of your confidence, but I knew you were not one to bluff. So, after I left, I couldn't get your stupid threats out of my mind. I decided to reduce your pain and end you today itself but imagine my surprise when I found out that you have escaped. I know all about the recording Raj, and I suggest you hand it over to me really soon."

"Never."

"In that case you better be alert. My men could hurt you and your friends anytime. They are noobs, so it's quite possible that what was meant to simply scratch an arm, that bullet could kill you too. Beware."

Saying this he cut the call.

Raj was actually scared now. Not for himself but for his friend. He couldn't put their lives in danger, but he couldn't let a criminal like Pankit win either. What was he to do?

20

THE THREAT

Raj held Krutika's hand and pulled her back inside the house. He took her to his room. Krutika could tell from his expressions that it was a serious matter and didn't ask any questions. Once they were inside the room, Raj locked the door and shut and covered all the windows. Everyone was perplexed. They could not understand the reason behind his actions. When he was done, he sat on the bed looking very tense. Seeing him stressed, Seena sat straight carefully placing her foot on the ground. She looked at Rohit and Krutika who were just as surprised as she was. She held Raj's face and made him look at her. She took hold of his hands and looked into his eyes.

"Shadow, calm down. Take deep breaths. Whatever is worrying you, forget about it for a second and just focus on me, okay?"

Raj nodded and did as she said.

"Good, now do you remember why you had given me the nickname, Light? Can you repeat it?"

"Yes, I had given you the nickname Light because Shadow cannot exist without a source of Light. And since you call me Shadow, it only made sense for me to call you Light. You are the light of my life."

Seena smiled. "Amazing. Do you feel better?"

"Yes, I am much calmer now. Thank you."

"My pleasure."

"Seena, how did you manage to calm him?" Rohit was curious.

"Simple. I made block out all the thoughts that were clouding up his head and made him focus on just one thing, me. Then, I gave his brain an activity to do that was related to me, so that I could make sure that his focus was not divided. Once he did that, his head cleared as he wasn't thinking about everything at the same time. And when I appreciated him for his response and confirmed if he felt better that moment, I broke the focus, and he was gently able to regain his composure." Seena clarified.

"Well done, Angel" Krutika praised her.

"Thanks Kruts. Now Raj, will you tell us what happened and why are you back so soon?" Seena inquired.

Raj looked at the three of his friends as he sighed. He looked at Seena's foot and gently placed it on his lap again, as she laid back. Then he began, "I got a call. It was from Pankit. He knows Light and I have escaped. He knows about the recording too. He threatened me that if I didn't give the pen drive to him, he will hurt us and he isn't afraid to kill us, if need be. I denied giving the recording to him for now, but I don't know what to do next. We could be attacked anytime, anywhere. It is not safe to go to the police for now because if we do, our lives will be in danger, and I can't take that risk. However, I cannot just give up either. He is a criminal, and I am a lawyer, I cannot let him win. I don't know what to do now."

Everyone was quiet for a few minutes. It would be an understatement to say they were shocked. They were terrified.

"Don't worry my brother. I am sure we will think of something. Fow now, it's best if none of us get out of the house. Angel, you don't have any surgeries scheduled for today, do you?" Rohit broke the silence.

"No, I do not, thankfully. And Devil is right. We will find a solution, Shadow, I promise you." Seena replied.

"Thanks guys. I am just really worried." Raj tried to smile a bit.

"Don't be. We are here for you. Whatever happens we will face it together, as a team." Krutika assured him.

Raj felt a little better after his friends consoled him.

"Umm, guys, I will be back. Just a minute." Krutika said and left.

She went to a different room and called someone. "Hey dad"

"Hello sweetie. How are you?"

"I am fine. How are you?"

"I am also good. What happened? Why did you call?"

"Can you hold a meeting with the Singhanias and the Malhotras soon?"

"Sure, but why?"

"You will know in the meeting itself. So please just manage that and also try to keep it as soon as possible, like tomorrow itself."

"Okay, but what reason should I give?"

"Anything, like maybe you can say that you want to see the sample product or that you want to know the progress report, anything. Inform them immediately. Okay?

"Fine with me. How is your boyfriend by the way?"

"He is fine. You will meet him in the meeting. I promise."

"Great, can't wait. See you soon. Bye princess."

"Bye. Love you."

"Love you too." Krutika finished her call and went back to the others. They were still thinking about how they could expose Pankit without risking their safety. Suddenly Raj's phone rang. He picked it up as it was his client, Mr. Sharma.

"Hello sir. How are you today?"

"I am fine and hope you are too. Getting to the point, I have decided to hold a meeting at my company tomorrow, so that you can share the progress report with me. Also, the Singhanias are going to be present too."

"Sure sir, we'll be there. Thank you."

"Okay, see you then. Bye."

"Bye sir."

The moment he put the phone down, Rohit asked, "Was it Mr. Sharma?"

"Yes" Raj answered.

"What did he say?" Rohit questioned.

"He said that he is going to hold a meeting for us tomorrow so that we can show him our progress report." Raj was smiling.

"That's great then. It gives us an opportunity to show him the recording." Seena announced.

"Yes, but we need to keep the recording in a safe place till then." Raj warned.

"True. Here is the pen drive. I suggest you tie it around your wrist as a bracelet with the help of a piece of rope. That way it won't get lost." Rohit advised.

"Right, good idea, but I think it is better if I wear it as a locket instead. I have some chains from my old lockets. I will bring them." Raj went out of the room. Soon he came back with a chain in his hand. He inserted the pen drive in his chain and wore it.

"Perfect. Now all of us should get some rest. It's going to be a long day tomorrow." Seena spoke.

"Right. Okay, Seena, you and Kruts can share this room, while Raj and I can sleep in his room tonight." Rohit decided.

The others were happy with the arrangement. They spent some time together and planned on leaving early for the meeting. Though everything was settled, they couldn't sleep well that night because of the anxiety and anxiousness that they felt.

The next morning, all four of them left as planned. They hadn't told their parents about anything as they didn't want them to get worried. They didn't even take the Malhotras' driver anywhere, so that they could keep it a secret.

On their way to the meeting, Raj's car ran out of fuel and stopped working. He was confused as he was supposed to have a full tank. He got out and checked. He found that the tank had been leaking. They were stranded in the middle of the road. There were no other cars there, as they had taken a shortcut to reach quickly.

21

THE TRUTH IS OUT

Raj tried to call someone for help but there was no signal in his phone. He informed the others and went a bit further from the car trying to catch a network. When he finally got the signal, he dialed his driver's number but before he could place the call, someone pushed him from behind, took off his locket and ran away. By the time that Raj could get up and comprehend the action, the person was nowhere in sight. Realizing with horror that their only piece of evidence was gone, he fell to the floor again. He let his tears out, crying at having lost the battle of justice. He got up and called his driver. After the call, he walked back dejectedly to the car. As she saw him returning, Seena noticed his upset face and got out of the car and ran up to him. She held his shoulders as he looked into her eyes, his tears still flowing out from his eyes and onto his cheeks. He hugged her and started crying on her shoulder. Her heart broke, seeing him like this. She tried to console him, but nothing worked. She pulled out of the hug, held him by his waist, with his hand around her neck and dragged him to the car. She sat him in the back and got on her knees in front of him. He looked at her as she held his hand.

"What happened Shadow? Why are you crying? You know you can tell me, right? I will never judge you. Please tell me what happened otherwise how will I help you? Please."

"We lost; we lost Light. Pankit won. One of his men pushed me and took the locket with him. We lost the only proof we had. We are doomed. And it's all because I wasn't careful. Stupid me." Raj kept crying.

"It's okay. We got the proof once; we will get it again. If not now, then some other day, we will defeat him. I promise you. And it's not your fault. You weren't expecting him to come after you on this deserted road too. Don't blame yourself. He is the criminal, he should be the one crying and begging in front of you, not the other way around. Stop crying now. It will all be fine. For now, we have to attend the meeting too, right? We can't miss it. Whatever happens, we will face it together. Don't worry." Seena comforted him.

The others also tried their best to calm him down and they were successful. Seena kissed Raj's forehead and said, "You stay in the back and try to relax. I will drive. My foot is better now after you iced it yesterday. Okay?'

The driver reached the spot and was instructed to wait by the car. Raj had already called the mechanic too when he had asked the driver to come. He was in tears but was still in senses.

The four left for the meeting again, but this time Seena was driving. When they reached, neither of them felt the excitement that they had yesterday, but Krutika wasn't so upset. As they were about to go in, Rohit got a message. It was from Pankit. He had sent a video in which he was crushing their pen drive under his car. The four could barely control their pain. They gathered up the courage and went inside. They were welcomed by Mr. Sharma and Pankit in the meeting room.

Rohit went up to Mr. Sharma "Hello Mr. Sharma. How do you do?"

"I am fine. What about you, Rohit? How are you feeling now?"

"I am feeling much better, thanks to Dr. Seena over there. Thank you for asking."

The other three came towards them as Seena's name was mentioned.

"Hello Mr. Sharma. Good morning." Raj greeted him.

"Good morning to you too Raj. And who are these beautiful ladies?" Mr. Sharma asked.

"Hello sir, I am Dr. Seena, I am a surgeon by profession, but I am well-versed in the field of business too. I help Raj and Rohit in their company." Seena introduced herself.

"I am Krutika, a dentist by profession. I am Rohit's girlfriend. I too help them out from time to time." Krutika told him.

"Good to know. Welcome to my company, all of you. Now I know, this meeting is quite sudden, and I am sorry for the short notice, but I have my reasons for it." Mr. Sharma apologized.

"It's no problem, sir." Raj assured him.

Pankit came up to them.

"Sir, I think we should begin the meeting now."

"Sure. So, Mr. Pankit, what is the progress report of your company?" Mr. Sharma asked as everyone seated themselves.

"The report is excellent sir. Infact, I think that you should entrust us with the complete order. With the accident and Mr. Rohit's love life involved, the order would be a burden on them, sir. I assure you that I can give you an impressive quality of work within a short span of time. Just give me like a few weeks extra, sir. I will complete the whole order in just two months. We should be considerate of Mr. Malhotra and his family too. Afterall, they are the best in the industry." Pankit explained his point of view while smirking at the four friends.

"Hmm. What do you say, Raj?" Mr. Sharma questioned him.

Before he could say a word, Krutika spoke up.

"Sorry for interrupting Mr. Sharma, but I would like to ask you something before you move ahead. Would you like to work with a criminal who deserves to rot in prison?"

Everyone was shocked. They had no evidence, so accusing Pankit can be seen as an act of defamation.

"What are you saying? I am not a criminal, you get that." Pankit shouted at Krutika, but she was unbothered.

"Did I mention your name, Mr. Pankit? I don't think so, then why are you getting so worked up?" Krutika raised her eyebrows.

Pankit was silent as he didn't know what to say. Mr. Sharma decided to take control of the situation.

"No, I would never consent to work with a criminal who must be punished by law. Why did you ask?"

"I think Mr. Pankit's extreme reaction just now is enough of an answer to that question. Still, I would like to show you something. If I may?" Krutika asked for permission.

"You may" Mr. Sharma allowed her.

She went to the projector and took out a pen drive from socks. She inserted it into the computer and played the recording that was done by Seena and Raj.

Everyone's expressions changed as they saw the video. Raj, Seena and Rohit were both happy and surprised, Mr. Sharma was angry, and Pankit was scared. When the video ended, Mr. Sharma turned to Pankit and screamed at him.

"What is this? So, you lied to me, to the world and you tried to kill Raj, Rohit and Seena. How dare you? You don't deserve any contract. She is right, you deserve to rot in prison and nothing else."

"Told you dad" Krutika smirked.

Everyone was even more astonished when Krutika called Mr. Sharma as dad and hugged him.

"I am sorry princess, but next time tell me before only. Okay sweetie?"

"Yes dad, I promise." She accepted.

"DAD?" Everyone except Mr. Sharma and his daughter shouted at the same time.

"Yes guys, Mr. Sharma is my dad. I am Krutika Sharma, right?"

Then it clicked for them. Krutika was Mr. Sharma's daughter.

"Sorry for not telling you before, but I actually wanted to keep it a secret. I don't like to boast about my dad, and I didn't want to receive special treatment from all of you. I wanted to be independent too. So, I had to hide it. I am sorry" Krutika tried to explain herself.

Her friends forgave her. Suddenly the police entered.

"Someone named Ms. Krutika had called?", said the lieutenant.

"Yes, that's me and that guy, Pankit is the one you have to arrest. I have the proof with me. He lied about his company's financial condition and tried to kill all my friends." Krutika told the officer the whole story and played the video for him. Then she gave him the pen drive.

"Thank you miss." The officer thanked her.

After the officer left with Pankit in arrest, everyone turned to Krutika. She saw everybody looking at her and knew they deserved an explanation.

"Okay, I know you all are wondering what just happened. I will tell you everything. To begin with I am Krutika Sharma, the daughter of Mr. Sharma who is not only the manager, but also the owner of KS Companies. And KS actually refers to my initials. As for Pankit, well we already know what he did and why, so I knew that if he can attempt to kill us once, there is no way he won't try again. When Raj told us about his threat, I called my dad and asked him to arrange this meeting. I knew that if I kept the meeting today, Pankit won't try to harm us. However, I was also aware that he would try to steal the pen drive at least. As a precaution, last night, when everyone was asleep, I made a duplicate copy of the pen drive and replaced it with the original one. So, the drive I gave the officer just now was the original copy. Dad, I did not tell all this to you beforehand because I wanted to expose him with the evidence. If I had simply warned you, he would have accused us of defamation, or he could have tried his tricks with someone else. The best way to get rid of him was to hand him over to the police. And I did just that. I planned on playing this recording here today, so I called the police too. They were a bit late, and I had to play it again but that's alright. I know all of you were so dejected after the pen drive was stolen. Raj couldn't stop crying. I am really sorry for hiding the truth from all of you, but I wanted to surprise you. I wanted to see you happy and shocked faces. I hope you understand."

Nobody said a word. Krutika was beginning to feel nervous because of the silence. Rohit noticed her anxiety and said, "Queenie, you don't need to be nervous. None of us are upset with you. Infact, we are so proud of you that we have no words to praise you. You did what all of us combined couldn't do. I am truly a lucky man, to have you in my life. Thank you for everything. I love you."

Krutika blushed and everyone smiled at the sight.

"Devil is right Kruts. All of us are extremely impressed. Honestly, we should have thought of making a duplicate copy, but we didn't, and you did. Well done, my bestie. You know what? You are the real Angel for you saved us all today." Seena praised her.

They all chuckled, except for Mr. Sharma.

"Kruts, you are our savior. Not kidding, but Rohit really is very lucky. You are smart, talented and beautiful. I don't have enough words to express the gratitude that I feel right now. Mr. Sharma, I would like to say one thing to you. You raised a perfect daughter. I am sure you are proud of her too. Thank you so so so much, Kruts." Raj thanked her.

"You are absolutely right Raj. I am very proud to have my princess as my daughter. I can raise my head with pride and say that my daughter is an excellent dentist, businesswoman and detective too. Not to forget a great daughter, friend and girlfriend." Mr. Sharma was really proud of his daughter.

Krutika was all shy by now.

"Thank you everyone for understanding me. I am really blessed to have you all in my life." She expressed her gratitude.

The room was full of smiles. All of them hugged Krutika one by one.

22
THE LOVE STORIES

Rohit looked at Krutika and signaled her to officially introduce him to her dad. She understood and took him near her father.

"Dad, you already know that Rohit is my boyfriend. I told you; you will meet him today. I don't need to clarify anything, as I have told you everything about him. He is the guy I have loved since college. We started dating back then but even when it ended, we never lost touch. Both of us were busy making our careers so we couldn't meet each other, but we always had long video calls, and a million messages. We maintained a long-distance relationship, even if we lived in the same city. I guess we just got so used to the calls and our daily routine, we weren't in a hurry for a change. Anyways, now we are together. And I know you have accepted him. So just give us your blessings, please." Krutika recounted everything that she needed to.

"Rohit. I have always known you are a great guy, and I don't think I can ask for a better son-in-law. I know you love my daughter by the way you call her queen. True, she is my princess and your queen. As long as you abide by that, I have no problems with your relationship. If you ask me, you may as well get married, and I will support you in your decision." Mr. Sharma was happy.

"Thank you, sir. It really means a lot. I promise you, she will always be my Queenie, no matter what." Rohit said looking at the love of his life.

"Just call me uncle. You too, Raj and Seena." Mr. Sharma objected.

"Yes, uncle." The three said in unison.

Later on, the four of them left for their own homes. Everyone was really relieved and happy, but the Malhotra brothers were thinking something. The next day Rohit called Seena and invited her to his house whereas Raj asked to meet Krutika in a cafe.

With Rohit and Seena, Seena came to his house and called for him. A servant told her that he was in the backyard. She went there and found him sitting idle, deep in thought.

"Devil, what happened? Why do you look so down?" Seena asked, pulling him out of his thoughts.

He looked at her. "Angel, do you remember what Queenie's dad said to me yesterday? That he would be happy even if we decided to get married."

"Yeah, I remember. Isn't that a good thing? Why are so tensed?"

"It's just that I realized that if Kruts and I got married, she would have to take care of me her whole life. You know, as well as I do, that I can never walk again. I am disabled. Yet neither her nor her dad have any problems with it. I am touched but it makes me feel inconsiderate. I can't be a burden on the girl I love. I know she will never complain, but it will be tough for her. She might get teased and taunted for having a differently abled husband. I can't bear for her to go through that pain. I love her too much to make her struggle because of me."

"Aw, my Devil. You really don't need to worry. Love is not a burden on anyone. And the fact that you are even worrying about his shows how much you love and care for her. Trust me, your emotions, your love, your care, is more than enough for her to be happy for the rest of her life. She loves you for you, not for your body. Initially, I was also doubtful but when I asked her, she was confident that she does not care about how you look, or if you can't walk. As long as you love her, the way you did in college and up until now, she is the luckiest girl in the world. She is more than excited to be your wife one day. She is always going to say yes, whenever you propose her. I promise you."

"Thank you, Angel. You are right, I was overthinking it. She loves me and I love her and that's all that matters. Who cares what the world has to say? Our love is ours, not the world's."

"Exactly. And I suggest that you propose her soon, so that I can play with me niece or nephew as soon as possible."

"ANGEL, control your emotions. There is a lot of time for that." Rohit couldn't stop blushing.

Seena laughed. "Okay fine. Anyway, I got to go now. I have to perform a surgery in an hour. See you. Bye. Don't forget to tell me how your proposal went."

"Okay I won't. Bye. See you and all the best."

"Thanks."

Seena left for the hospital.

On the other side, with Raj and Krutika. They met in a café near Raj's office. They sat down and after they had placed their orders, Raj began.

"Kruts, you are probably aware that I am in love with Seena. I am not a huge fan of nicknames, but I didn't mind her giving me one. Infact, I gave her one too. When I saw her being all touchy and flirting with Pankit in the restaurant, I was so jealous, even though I was the one who had asked her to do it. When her foot got stuck under that sumo, I was so worried. I couldn't bear to see her in pain. And when I am stressed, or cannot think straight, she knows how to calm me down. I really love her, and I want to propose to her, but I don't know how. Can you give me any ideas? You are her best friend after all."

"Sure, why not? Firstly, I don't think you should ask her to be your girlfriend."

"What, why?"

"You should ask her to be your wife instead. You both are at a stage where you can get married without any fuss. Your careers are thriving, so it's better that your love life does too."

"Are you sure?"

"Yes, yes, I am. I know she would want that too."

Their coffee arrived.

"Okay but how do I propose her?" Raj questioned.

"Just do one thing, be yourself. Put in the effort, do what you think she likes, get a ring that reminds you of her, make it an unforgettable moment. You don't need to spend much money on it, it's the effort and thought that counts. Try your best and don't panic. No matter what, she will say yes, because she loves you too. I have seen it in her eyes. And make sure it comes as a surprise to her. She loves surprises. Other than that, you can work out the details on your own because the proposal and the preparations should come from you, from your heart. They should depict your love for her. So, I won't be helping you with that." Krutika advised.

"I understand. Thank you for your advice. I promise I will make it the best day of her life."

"You better."

That night, Rohit was jotting down ideas on how to propose to Krutika, when Raj came into his room to discuss a case he was working on. He saw him writing and sneaked up on him to scare him. However, when he reached near Rohit, he saw the list of ideas and realized what it meant.

"No way", he said a little loudly.

Rohit got a jump scare and turned around. He relaxed when he saw that it was just his brother.

"What?", Rohit asked.

"You are planning on proposing to Krutika. Aren't you?'

"Yeah, and? What's the problem with that?"

"There is none, but the thing is I am also proposing to Seena, for marriage."

"There's no way. Are you serious?"

"Absolutely serious."

"Wow. We think alike, huh?"

"We really do. I mean we are brothers after all."

"True. So, what's your plan? How exactly are you proposing to her?"

"To be honest I didn't really have a plan yet, but I think I do now. And if you agree, we can propose together.'

"That'd be awesome. What's the idea?"

Raj told him his idea, which Rohit loved. They decided to act upon it the upcoming weekend. Then they discussed the case Raj had come for and once they were done, Raj left the room.

The following weekend, the brothers invited the two girls to a picnic on a beach located on the outskirts of the city.

They all carried a change of clothes with them, as they planned on going to a 5-star restaurant for dinner after the picnic.

At the beach, they set up a blanket, placed their things and started enjoying their time together, having fun, splashing water at each other, chasing after one another, having the time of their lives.

As the sun was about to set, the sky started to form a beautiful view.

"Kruts, Light, why don't you both go ahead and get changed? We will pack up till then. There is a guesthouse on out right side." Raj suggested.

"Are you sure, Shadow? You guys need to change too." Seena was doubtful.

"We will go after you come back. And yes, we are sure. You should go now." Rohit pushed the idea.

"Okay, if you say so. Come on Angel, let's go." Krutika agreed.

The two girls took their clothes and went to change. They got dressed up beautifully and returned after 15 minutes.

"We are back, you should go get changed now. We will be here watching the sunset. Okay?" Seena told the boys.

"Okay, we will be back. Bye." Raj said and left with Rohit in tow.

Seena and Krutika focused on the beautiful scene in front of them. With the sun setting, the sky turned a beautiful shade of red, which combined with the blue of the sea formed such a heavenly sight.

Behind them, Raj and Rohit had already come back. They were really quiet as they laid down a beautiful white cloth and covered it with rose petals. They set up a camera nearby to record them. They took a rose each out of their bags and got down on one knee, right behind their girls.

"We are back", they shouted in unison.

The girls looked back and were astonished. Before they could even say a word, Raj and Rohit proposed.

"Light, I know this is probably coming as a huge surprise to you, but I don't think it's completely unexpected. I mean I think we both know by now how we feel about each other. We haven't known each other for that long, but I really cannot imagine myself without you by my side anymore. You have been with me through thick and thin. You made me calm down when I was stressed. I never cried, but when I did, you were the first one to notice. You held my hands and comforted me. Even at the beginning, when you stood up to me, I was more impressed than angry. When you were accused of crimes you didn't do, I felt it in me that you were innocent. When you flirted with someone else, I was jealous. Over the past few weeks, we have become closer than I ever thought was possible. You have saved my life, and I have helped you with your pain. You understood me better than anybody. That time when you asked why I gave you the name Light, I said it was because I was Shadow. It was because you are the light of my life and without you, I am incomplete. I am weak. I really love you Seena and so I want to ask you to not only be my partner, but also my life partner. Will you marry me, my love?", Raj confessed.

Seena had tears in her eyes listening to his confession. She was speechless. She was too happy to even express. All she could do was nod her head, indicating that her answer was a yes. She accepted the rose and Raj got up to give her a hug and a peck on the forehead.

"I love you too, my Shadow. And I know you will never leave my side because as long as there is light, somewhere, there will be shadow too. Thank you for being there for me. You carried me when I couldn't walk. You trusted me to help with your business when you barely knew me. I know I am lucky to have you and I am so glad about that fact. If there is anyone for me, it's you. Let's get married." Seena was getting emotional.

Raj simply smiled and engulfed her in his embrace. Rohit and Krutika were looking at them and were feeling touched by their confessions. Then they looked at each other.

"I don't think I need words to express my love for you. We have been together for years now. It started out as college love but now it's much more than that. Even when college ended, we couldn't separate. We kept in touch all those years. Not all long- distance relationships work but ours did, because we made it work. No matter what happened, you were there for me. I lost my legs, yet I didn't lose you and I think that's my biggest achievement. Thank you so much for loving a guy like me. Words really cannot express my feelings for you. I was afraid that I would be a burden on you after marriage, but as per your own words that you spoke to Seena, your love is way bigger than any problem you could possibly face. I love how you care, not only for but for others too. You saved us yesterday. You have done so much for us, for me, that I cannot thank you enough. All I know is that I would be a fool to not propose even after all these years and all those moments that we spent together, the memories that we made. So here I am, asking you to marry me. Will you accept being called my wife?' Rohit popped the question.

Krutika just accepted the rose in his hand and said, "Trust me, pleasure is all mine. Where else would I find a guy who calls me his queen as a pet name. One who loves me so much. Who is more worried about my struggles than his own. I am such a lucky girl to have found you. Our love has blossomed in beautiful ways, and I couldn't ask for more. I would really love nothing more than to have you as my husband and become your wife."

She bent down to hug Rohit as they both let out tears of joy.

"So cute, but when did you both plan all of this?" Seena questioned.

"After we talked to the both of you. Raj found out that I was going to propose to Krutika, so he suggested that we do it together." Rohit explained.

Raj played a romantic song. "Now, it's time to officially make you both our fiancés"

Both Raj and Rohit took out a ring and put it on the ring finger of their respective girls.

"It is beautiful. Thank you." Seena whispered.

"Not more beautiful than you." Raj replied making Seena blush.

"I love it, my love" Krutika said.

"I love you more" Rohit answered.

"By the way, Raj, remember I told you I was predicting the future?" Rohit reminded his brother.

"Yes, you were right. Amazing skills. I am impressed." Raj praised him.

"You better be." Rohit laughed.

The two couples spent the rest of the evening together, laughing, chatting, clicking pictures and making memories. They had dinner in the restaurant and enjoyed their time.

EPILOGUE: Raj completed his order in time and was praised by everyone in the textile industry for his heroic deeds. His parents found out everything and were very proud of him. Rohit gained the confidence to join work again and continued fighting cases in the court of law and justice. Krutika and Seena were happy in both their professional and love lives. Pankit confessed to his crimes and was punished with life imprisonment. Everything was well and good in life.

"Love and friendship are gifts of life. They might not come when you expect them but when you have them, you cherish them."

The End